GRAVE NEW WORLD

GRAVE NEW WORLD

DOWN & DIRTY SUPERNATURAL CLEANING SERVICES BOOK 1

KATE KARYUS QUINN DEMITRIA LUNETTA
MARLEY LYNN

CONTENTS

For Marley Lynn who really wanted to title one of the books in this series Madame Ovary.

And for Demitria - who will never let her do it.

But mostly for Kate, who doesn't believe in false modesty and is really and truly indispensable due to her formatting of all books, making of covers, and general excellence of character.

Sign up for our newsletter to receive FREE short stories!
Visit www.marleylynn.com/newsletter

Like us on Facebook for books deals, surprise sales, and promotions!
www.facebook.com/MarleyLynnAuthor

Cleaning up after a vampire rave sucks.

Pun intended.

My first one, I came armed with a whole truckload of hydrogen peroxide, expecting blood stains everywhere. In my mind, they covered the walls and floors and ceilings. I expected something like what a plasma donation center would look like if it was run by someone hopped up on way too much Mountain Dew.

It turns out, though, that vampires are not messy eaters. You might even say they don't like to waste a single drop of their meal. It's sacred to them the way Ho-Ho's were to my seventh-grade math teacher.

So yeah, it's not the prospect of scrubbing away blood stains that's getting me down as I drive through the warehouse district searching each building for the 6669 the vamps paint on the wall of their chosen party spot. The number's some sort of vampire humor, I think. Or maybe not. They're hard to read and I'm not interested in getting close enough to find out anything about them beyond that they pay in cash.

"Where is this stupid place?" I ask aloud, even though there's no one else in the van with me. Although...my van is kind of sentient. Like a cross between Christine and Herbie, it's both terrifying and adorable.

Vanna was stolen ages ago. Back when she...er, *it*, was just a normal Grand Caravan with stained seats and a dented back fender from some tailgating asshole. I figured that was the last I'd see of it, but a few months back I opened my door and there was Vanna (yes, I named her and yes I hate myself for it). The same...but also totally different.

I would've sent her straight back to the impound lot where she was found if it wasn't for the fact that I was desperate for transportation. The transmission had just died on my previous van and without wheels I had no job. So I used Vanna, figuring I could just pretend she was normal. Just another vehicle.

That didn't last long.

In response to my question, Vanna takes over steering, which is always annoying. But I forgive her as she parks us in front of a building, the 6669 on the wall straight ahead.

From the outside the warehouse looks totally unremarkable. Just another big boxy building. I can't hold back a big sigh as I grasp the handles on the giant sliding door. Putting all my weight into it, I pull the door hard. With a groan it gives way, gliding open and allowing a bright shaft of sunlight to cut through the dark interior.

"Aw fuck," I say as a giant water tank fills my vision. I'm not talking about some little pet store thing; this is Sea World size. I have no idea how I'm gonna drain this thing and scrub it spotless. That's the job, though. I'm supposed to leave only the dust motes and a sparkling clean tank behind when I'm done.

This alone would be a monumental task, but as I walk

into the warehouse and closer to the tank and the moving shadows within, I know it's gonna get worse.

And it does.

Sharks. Big ones, too. They glide through the water with silent menace.

Those asshole vamps decided to have an underwater rave and feed on fucking sharks.

I thought the lions were the worst. Before that, I thought the pigs were the worst.

Clearly, I was wrong all those times. Because really, vampires are the worst. Always and forever—they are The. Worst.

I take a minute to swear viciously and creatively, cursing not just vampires but all the paranormal creatures that decided to come out of hiding a decade ago and totally screw up everything. Sometimes I hear people say that it's better to know than to live in ignorance. I disagree. The time when I believed that werewolves, harpies, and faeries were all just stories was a great time. An easier, simpler one too.

I was only in my early twenties when everything changed. My dad's cleaning business was struggling and I'd just graduated with a degree in English that I was quickly realizing was pretty much useless in the real world. Then we had a little apocalypse. Cities disappeared beneath the sea. Crops failed. And all the supes came out to play. Suddenly college degrees didn't mean much. Survival was our entire focus.

I got married to my boyfriend, 'cause it felt like we might all die and I guess I wanted to wear a white dress first? I don't know. It wasn't the greatest decision. I also went into business with Dad. But we revamped it. Pun intended.

Harper Cleaning became Down & Dirty: Supernatural Cleaning Services. Dad said we were kinda like the clean-up crew for the Ghostbusters. "Think about it," he'd say. "Someone had to mop up that marshmallow mess, and I bet they got paid good money. Hazard pay, right?"

He was right. The business thrived. My marriage failed. But overall, life was good.

Until my parents disappeared along with a few hundred thousand other folks.

But that's another story.

Right now, I gotta figure out how to get these sharks outta this tank.

Luckily, we're in the Newark Port district. I understand now why they chose this location. But still, the Bay is a good ten minutes away. Can a shark survive that long out of water?

Pulling out my phone, I start to Google.

Some people might think I'm just a cleaning lady, but in truth, this job requires way more than just a mop and broom.

Yesterday I was choking on feathers cleaning out a frat house that had been full of chicken shifter strippers. Today I'm wrestling sharks. Tomorrow I might be scrubbing harpy droppings off some vocal Humans First protester's roof and lawn.

Down & Dirty is more than just a job. It's a lifestyle.

2

─────

I t's nearly midnight by the time I get back to the office. I'm soaking wet and stink like a can of tuna fish. The knuckles on my right hand ache from punching a shark in the face. It was necessary—those sharks were hungry and thought I might be a tasty afternoon snack. It was good to know my right hook works even underwater, but I didn't have time to ice it afterwards and now I'm paying for it.

Overall, it wasn't a great day.

But I did return those damn sharks to the sea and get that tank emptied. So technically it's a win. It just doesn't quite feel that way.

I wouldn't even bother going back to the office, except that I want to bill the vamps for the cherry picker with power lift, rescue harness, and ten miles of tubing to empty the tank. No way am I paying the interest on that shit if they don't pony up before my credit card bill is due.

The street is mostly dark. This is the type of town where the sidewalks get rolled up at nine and noise ordinances are strictly enforced. The only person still open is my business neighbor, Eye Wide Open Private Investigations. The dude is a giant werewolf with an eyepatch, so that's meant to be clever. The first time we met I told him it was "punny" and he replied that puns are the lowest form of humor. Clearly we don't see eye to eye. Pun abso-fucking-lutely intended.

I'm not gonna take tips on what is and is not funny from this guy. I think he used up any and all humor he possesses on his business name 'cause everything about Nico is dark and scary. Maybe, if I'm being honest, also a little bit sexy too. In that bad boy kind of way that my ex really should've cured me of finding attractive ever again. But my ex was bad in a prankster kind of way, whereas Nico has more of a quiet smolder thing going on.

I don't like it. And I don't like him. If a past client wasn't giving me a deal on the rent, I'd move just to get away from him. For now, though, I'm stuck with him.

Before sitting at my desk, I pull a beer out of the minifridge squeezed between my two filing cabinets. If anyone asks I say that it's to keep my lunch salads fresh. But let's be honest, some days require a cold beer at the ready. And this is definitely one of them.

Twisting the cap off, I collapse into my desk chair and then boot up my laptop. Twenty minutes later I'm just finishing up the invoicing when the bell on the door jingles, alerting me that a customer is entering the shop. Only problem is...I definitely locked the door.

I spin and roll my chair out from behind the wall of plants I use for privacy. I never had a green thumb until I inherited an aggressive Venus fly trap. The Venus fly trap was inside Vanna when she was returned to me, with a note beside her that said, *Please take care of my Vee, she prefers white mice.*

Now I swear the fly trap actually hisses as a tall skinny man steps through the doorway and into the shop.

"Stop right there," I demand, reaching for the only weapon I have close at hand—a broom.

He smiles slightly and his eyes dance with humor. The light is low, but there's also a glowy quality to him. Which means this guy is either very into a gold-based skincare routine—or he's fae.

I'm betting on the latter.

"I come in peace," he says, laughter in his voice.

I point to the door with the very obvious closed sign. "That door was locked and these are not my business hours. Come in peace tomorrow."

He shrugs. "I suppose I could find another cleaning service, however, you come highly recommended. And since I'm being intrusive by showing up outside of regular business hours, I'll pay you double your rate."

"You don't even know what my regular rate is," I say.

"It doesn't matter. I'll pay it. And..." He reaches into the bag I hadn't even noticed slung across his shoulder. It lies flat against his hip, but somehow he pulls out a huge package wrapped in white butcher paper. "Prime steaks. Share them with your friends and family. A rare treat, I'm sure."

Ugh, I hate him. And hate the way my mouth is watering. He's right; steaks are a rare treat these days. The whole crops failing because of the apocalypse thing was not great for the food supply. While chicken, beef, and pork used to be staples on our table, these days beans and rice are way more common. The idea of a good seared steak is enough to make my stomach grumble.

"What's the job?" I ask.

"I've recently come into some property. I believe it was

unoccupied for some time. It's rundown and a bit…undesirable at the moment. I need it cleaned up."

I frown. "That doesn't sound like something for which you'd be willing to pay double."

His steady smile becomes tighter. Hard. "Perhaps to *you* it doesn't."

I take a minute to consider. My jobs for the next few days are for human clients, people who crossed swords with the supes and their property came out the worse for it. It's awful, but it's a lot easier to push them further down my schedule than it would one of my supernatural clients. As much as I hate them, they usually pay well and on time.

"Okay," I tell the fae guy. "I'll do it. Let me just get your information down."

I turn toward my desk for a pen and some paper, but he stops me with a single gesture, sliding forward with an almost liquid grace so that he's directly in front of me. "No need. Here's my card. The address is on the back. I should be on the premises, but if I'm not you may call me." He says 'call' with distaste. Supes are not good with modern technology.

As soon as I take the card, he covers his nose and quickly backs away, so he's not quite so close to the stink cloud surrounding me.

"Hold up," I say to him as I head back to my desk and grab the stack of business cards on top. In a moment of weakness, I splurged on the fancy kind. Thick paper, curved corners, and my own name on the back embossed. Paige Harper, Owner. I can never pick them up without running the pad of my thumb over those words.

Peeling one off the top, I stretch my arm far as it'll go so fae man doesn't have to enter the stink zone again. "Call me if anything changes."

"Nothing will," he assures me, taking the card. He examines it for a moment, then asks. "Ms. Harper?"

"That's me." I shrug. "I also answer to Paige, Hey you, and Cleaning lady."

"How...human," he says drolly. "My business here is concluded. I shall expect to see you at ten tomorrow morning," he adds, indicating the package of steaks and letting me know this meeting is over. Setting them on the small reception desk, he tips an imaginary hat and is gone as quickly and silently as he came.

As I turn back to my desk, I can't help but think that I'm getting too old for this shit. Sure, I just turned thirty-one, but this new supe-filled world seems to age us humans faster. Meanwhile, most of the supes appear to never age at all.

Raging at the unfairness of it all won't get me to my bed any faster.

Not that I'm in a hurry to get to my bed. There's not exactly someone in it waiting for me.

3

———

I'm wiped out, so I quickly finish up the invoice and email it. Vamps usually have a human or two doing their bidding, so I hope to get a big fat money transfer soon. Good thing too, because rent isn't going to just pay itself. And when your landlord is your ex-husband, you don't want to be late. And Jax never had a taste for red meat, so I don't think I can sucker him into letting me pay him with protein. But I'm not above trying.

Grabbing the steaks, I head out. But this shit-show of a day is not yet done. Nico, the private dick from next door, is waiting outside for me. I mean technically he's just leaning against the small slice of brick wall between our office doors, but the minute I walk out he turns my direction in a way that tells me he has something to say.

"Paige," he says, his voice a low rumbly growl that I feel in the pit of my stomach.

Ugh. I really can't stand him. He takes up more than his fair share of space, forcing me to step back or else just live with him standing uncomfortably close. At five foot nine, I'm not short, but next to Nico I feel petite. Maybe some girls would enjoy that feeling, but not me. The world is too uncertain and dangerous for me to indulge any damsel in distress fantasies. I may not be a supe, but I *am* a badass. And I like knowing that I can take care of myself.

Nico, though, seems to have the idea that I need his help and protection. More than once he's warned me from going into certain areas he deems too dangerous. Another time he mansplained to me how best to get animal hair off couch cushions. I mean, c'mon, dude. Sure, I get that he occasionally sheds, but I've been doing this job for a long time and don't need his helpful little tips.

In his eyes, I'm just a helpless human. Soft and easy prey for his kind—the supes of the world.

I hate being condescended to. And I hate supes. All of them.

I have lots of reasons, but the main one is The Great Ghosting. All around the world in one awful second hundreds of thousands people just—POOF!—disappeared. There and then gone. Just like that.

My parents were among them. Dad disappeared right before my eyes. One minute he had a slice of pizza in his hand and was complaining that Benny's was skimping on the pepperoni lately. "What's the world coming to when a man—"

He never finished that thought. Or his pizza.

The worst moment, though, was when I called Mom. She'd become addicted to her smartphone in recent years and even took it into the bathroom with her. I could always count on her to pick up on the first ring.

But on that day it went to voicemail.

And I knew then with a sick feeling in the depths of my stomach, that I'd never see her or Dad again.

And I haven't.

To this day there are no leads. No explanations. Nothing.

The supes swear up and down that they had nothing to do with it. That they lost many of their own.

It's true that supes disappeared too. But that doesn't absolve them from responsibility.

The supes have killed gods, causing earthquakes and tidal waves.

The supes have opened portals that release horrible monsters.

The supes bite off more than they can chew, and it's the normal people like me who suffer.

So yeah, I do business with supes cause a girl's gotta eat. But I don't trust, befriend, or sleep with them...anymore.

That being said...it has not escaped my attention that Nico is a very nice slice of manhood. Or half a slice, I guess. Since he's half wolf. But I've never seen that part of him—although sometimes on full moons if I work late I'll hear howling. It always makes all my hair stand on end.

Now he leans against the wall with his muscled arms folded across his broad chest. There's not one inch of flab on him. Trust me, I've looked. It's almost impossible not to. He wears these tight white tees and beat-up jeans. In the winter he adds a worn leather jacket. It's so cheesy. Like he's doing some sort of James Dean Rebel Without A Cause-type thing.

Except...oh man, it looks good on him. Real good.

So good that I have to sometimes remind myself that I would never get involved with a supe. I mean, I accidentally married a fae, but that was not my fault. He didn't even know he was fae, at the time. That was the first thing that soured me on supes, especially the attractive ones—and they *all* seem to be easy on the eyes.

But with Nico, sometimes I wonder what he might be like between the sheets. Maybe it's just my proximity to him.

Seeing him day in and day out. I noticed the other week when he changed his cologne.

Plus...the walls between our offices are thin. Like I've-heard-him-servicing-clients kind of thin. And by servicing, I mean that sometimes when ladies find out their husbands are cheating he comforts them with his penis. To be fair, the lady is always the one initiating it. But still, it happens enough that I know the sound Nico makes when he comes, so...

As if reading my mind, Nico says, "Thin walls round here, huh?"

"What?" I ask, jumping a little.

He frowns at me like he can't figure me out. "Heard you're doing work for a fae. You know who he is?"

I shrug. "No. Why should I?"

Nico points to my window.

It reads *Down & Dirty Supernatural Cleaning Services.* And there's my logo too. Dad hated it. Said he felt like he was prostituting me. But I insisted. Sex sells and we needed every advantage we could get. So there's a sex kitten cartoon that maybe if you squint could kinda look like me. Even Dad eventually had to admit—it worked. People walk by, see it, and stop. They read the window. Maybe they don't need us right now, but later when they get in a feud with the manticore family next door and get their lawn clawed to shreds—they remember me and call.

"You wanna be in the supernatural services?" Nico asks. "Then maybe you should know a little bit more about your clients."

"I know plenty," I counter. "And I don't need your warnings. I don't trust any of—" I just barely stop myself before I say 'you'—there's no need to make this personal. "My clients," I quickly correct.

But Nico knows exactly what I mean. He grins in a way that shows all his teeth. They're nice white, even teeth—not the yellowed fangs I'd expect. But still, there's something about them that feels more threatening than a normal human's collection of molars and canines. "Sure, I know. Like your boyfriend says, 'the only good supe is a dead supe.'"

I sigh. I hate when people bring this up. He said this a long time ago and has apologized for it. Also, he's not really my boyfriend anymore. He's either way more...or way less. But I'm not gonna get into all of that with Nico. I give him the short version. "That was a long time ago. Tensions were high. He said something on Twitter that he regretted. As head of the city council—"

"And future congressman," Nico interrupts.

I frown at this, but have to concede, "He's running, yes. And it's on a platform of tolerance and peace. It's not like he's with Humans First or anything. And for the record, neither am I."

Nico shakes his head, smiling "Oh, so it's good to know that you wouldn't outright kill me, given the chance. But a national database of all the supes, so that we can be watched—you support that?"

I throw my hands up. How did I know we were gonna end up having this argument? Again.

"It's not fair to humans if we don't know who is and is not a supe. Trust me, I was married to one and had no idea—"

Nico cuts me off with a wave of his hand. "Let's not do this. I didn't come out here to fight or"—he wrinkles his nose— "stand upwind of you for this long." I blush despite myself, really wishing I didn't smell so fishy. "I just wanted to tell you, I did work for that guy a long time ago. He's one of Oberon's lackeys. I wouldn't trust him. Not even a little bit."

"Who's Oberon?" I ask. "Some fae mob boss? Jimmy Hoffa with wings?"

"He's king of the fae. And not all fae have wings," Nico says. "In fact, only pixies—"

I can tell he's about to give me a whole species, family, genus breakdown for all of Faerieland, which I am 100% *not* interested in.

I cut him off before that can happen. "Yeah, don't care. All I need to know about the fae is that this one pays."

"Okay then..." Nico looks like he's gonna say more, but just shakes his head instead.

My inner voice is telling me that Nico's right. That fae dude, whose card had no name, just an address and phone number, is a big old mistake. Even with the bribe of fresh steaks. But there's no way I'm gonna admit that.

"I can take care of myself," I tell him.

"Can you?" he asks, his eyes moving from mine to something above us.

I duck instinctively, just as the *swoosh* of wings passes right over my head. A shriek escapes me, and I immediately hate myself for it. Before I have time to recoup, the harpy has wheeled back, and I'm familiar with the look in its eyes.

Harpies are ugly, but they are definitely some of the more peaceful supes. Or they *were*. But a few years back they discovered meth and suddenly their kind was no longer the poster child for human-supe relations. This one is amped up, and looking to take someone out. Specifically me. I don't know why. Maybe I look like the human that killed her sister. Maybe I look like the girl that stole her lover. Maybe I'm just the first unfortunate person she came across after she zoomed on Scooby Snax. Either way, I'm the target.

"Balls!" I scream, digging into the back of my pants. I keep my Ruger there. A good old-fashioned gun is useful on humans and supes alike, and I've flashed it in the faces of more than a few creeps. But there's a problem, and that problem is my vanity.

My pants are too tight.

The gods must've invented spandex because these leggings have been working hard all day keeping my tummy in and my tush tight. A lesser fabric would be sagging after the day I've put in, but these are still fighting the good fight.

Only problem is, right now they're not just holding my muffin top in, but my gun too.

I mean, I look hot as shit, but I'm also just about to be dead shit if I can't get the drop on this harpy. There's a snarl as the harpy dives, claws out, extended for my face.

Except it wasn't the harpy that growled. I realize that the second I'm hit by 200 pounds of man meat.

Oh...scratch that. Dog meat.

Nico has shifted, knocking me flat on my back. The harpy misses her prey and spins again to take a third pass. But Nico bares his teeth, emitting a deep, low growl. His chest vibrates on mine.

I can't claim that I hate it.

The harpy considers the challenge, then turns tail and wings away to the west. The massive werewolf on top of me jumps up, sniffs once at the sky to make sure the harpy is gone, and then he's Nico again, standing above me and offering a hand to help me up, his lip curled in a wry smile.

"I believe you were saying you could take care of yourself?"

I ignore the hand and scramble to my feet, brushing dirt

from my too-tight jeans. I always worried my pants would betray me, but I figured it would be with them splitting up the middle during a deep bend over. This, surprisingly, is worse.

Trying to preserve a little of my dignity, I stick my nose up in the air.

"Yes," I say, "I can." I turn my back to him, not even offering a thanks, and Vanna does the favor of opening the driver's side door for me, somehow knowing that I'm too shaken to do it myself.

But it's not the harpy attack that's got my nerves on edge.

Later, in bed, it's not the near miss from the harpy that replays in my mind. Instead, it's the moment Nico stood over me, fangs bared and his big dog dick swinging in my face. Not that it was a turn-on or anything. I'm not one of those human girls who wants to brag about getting banged by a bear. Nico's fur-covered hindquarters will never meet mine. But still, I can't help wondering...

Does Nico's human manhood have the same impressive hang as his wolf wang?

4

The next morning I wake to a rustling in the kitchen. The sounds and smells of someone putting together a five-star breakfast travel all the way up to my attic bedroom.

I kept the house in the divorce, and even though I love this place, I felt weird sleeping somewhere Jax and I christened during our deeply-in-love-let's-move-in-together stage. Turns out the only place we didn't bang was the attic, so I set up camp here while I redecorated the second-floor bedrooms.

It also has an unexpected bonus. A door that leads to one of those old-fashioned metal spiral staircases that takes you to a hatch in the roof and opens up to an amazing widow's walk. It's small—only a ten by ten square, but oh, the view! It didn't take long for me to discover that I liked the idea of staying up here, permanently.

But that doesn't answer who the hell is in my kitchen.

I grab my gun from under the mattress and walk down the stairs, putting my feet on just the right place for each step. I know these stairs like the back of my hand, and whoever is in here is going to be lucky if that's all I hit them with. The smell of frying meat reaches my nose and I consider just filling them with lead without asking any questions. Someone is cooking my steaks!

In my bare feet, I pad over to the kitchen entrance, then spin to draw a bead on the cut pair of shoulder blades laboring over my stove. I'd know them anywhere, and yes, they are nice. Too bad they belong to Jax, my shit-bird of a lying cheating fae ex-husband.

He turns, raises his eyebrows at the gun, then plates up the steaks. Three plates.

"You're not supposed to be here," I say. After a moment of hesitation, I lower the gun. This isn't the first time I've wanted to shoot Jax, and it's also not the first time I decided he wasn't worth the chunk of lead. "You don't live here anymore."

"It's still my house," he says.

"I'm paying you rent," I remind him. "You're technically my landlord. You can't just come in whenever you want."

I grab myself a cup of coffee. As I pass Jax, he plucks something from my temple.

"Is this...a fish scale?" he asks. "What kind of trouble have you gotten into?"

I scrub my hands through my hair, searching for any other fish bits that might've been left behind.

"None of your business." I tell him. "Now get out of my house."

"About that..." He sits at the table and tries to give me his award winning smile. That, and the memory of his shoulder blades under that t-shirt are almost enough to make me smile back. He's such a charming bastard, I have to remind myself that I hate him.

Brent is taller than Jax, Brent is taller than Jax. I say to myself as I take the place across from my ex. This happens sometimes when I'm around Jax. I just randomly start listing ways that my current flame is better than my former husband.

Brent has a real job. Brent pays his bills. Brent can tie his own tie. Brent has a future in politics. Brent—

The running diatribe breaks off as I make eye contact and Jax drops me a wink. I can't deny my attraction to Jax, still. That one wink and all I can remember is how good he was in the sack. I'm ashamed to admit how long our amazing sexuality compatibility outweighed all of Jax's less-than-awesome attributes. Like basically behaving like a frat boy 24/7. After all he's done to me, it really shouldn't take a lot of willpower to keep myself from climbing back into his bed. And yet it totally still does. Never mind that we've now been divorced for longer than we were ever married.

It's not fair. The marriage is supposed to last while attraction fades. Not the other way around.

"Do I smell breakfast?" An older man, maybe late fifties, strides in. "Are meals included in this deal?" he asks, his lips a straight line as he plops down on a chair beside me. Picking up my fork, he helps himself to a piece of steak.

"Who is this?" I ask, spinning toward Jax as alarm bells ring in my head. "What is going on here?"

"Well, you've been late on rent a few times..." Jax starts.

"But I always get it to you in the end. You can't evict me." He wouldn't. Would he?

I'm the one who found this house. Years before I knew Jax, I dreamed of living here. The stately old Victorian at the top of the hill. When Jax showed me the deed to the house and told me it was now ours...I cried. Big fat wet tears. I am not the crying type. But knowing this house was mine got me right in the tear ducts. Though it wasn't mine. It was Jax's.

His name on the deed. His property.

Now he holds his hands out placatingly. "I'm not evicting you. I'm just...leasing the ground floor bedroom."

My mouth drops open. "You can't..."

"Can and have, my dear," the old man tells me. "Jax here lost quite a lot of money to me last night and offered me a place rent-free for the next ten years. Can't say no to a deal like that."

"Ten years," I echo.

It all makes sense now. Jax loves to gamble. That's how he got this house in the first place, I eventually learned. "Paige, meet Darron." He gives my shoulder a squeeze. "You'll like him. He reminds me a little of your Pops."

"You brought me a replacement for my father, Jax?" I demand, unable to believe that I can be even angrier and yet here I am.

"Of course not! Nobody could replace him," Jax protests. "I'm just saying, I thought your Pops was the only man on earth who could successfully bluff me, but then this guy—" Jax gives Darron a hearty shake that must make his teeth rattle. "Got the best of me. Oh, and Darron, meet Paige. She's a bit prickly in the morning, but I'm sure you will get on swimmingly." There it is. That famous fae mischievousness. It's in the glint of his eyes and the curl of his lips.

"You rat bastard..." I start.

"Darron will be moving in today. It's all sorted."

I stare at the steaks, *my steaks*, feeling powerless. I've been here on my own for almost ten years. This. Is. My. Home.

When the roof leaked, I climbed up there and nailed on some new shingles. I know when the pipes are clanging in an 'everything is working fine' way or an 'uh-oh better call the plumber' kind of way. And when the plumber comes, I'm the one who pays him. If I leave it to Jax, he tries to DIY or call in someone who owes him a favor...and then makes everything worse.

Jax can't just give part of this house to someone else. A total stranger. Maybe even a supe. I turn to Darron, looking for some clue to whether he's human or something else. Something extra. No way am I house-sharing with a supe.

Darron takes his first bite of steak, makes a face, and spits it out.

Dabbing his lips with a napkin, he asks Jax, "Is this a joke?"

"I feel like this is all a joke," I say. "A bad one."

I take a big bite of steak, wondering if maybe he's a vamp and prefers his meat raw. The flavor hits me and I gag in surprise.

The steak has the same taste as cotton candy. No worse, it's like cotton candy flavored jelly beans. No...it's like cotton candy jelly bean-flavored vodka. Sickly sweet with an unnatural aftertaste.

"What the hell?" I say, reaching for my coffee, desperate to get the residue out of my mouth. "What did you do?" I ask Jax.

"I didn't put anything on them except salt and pepper!" Jax cries out. He tastes the steaks, closes his eyes and moans in bliss. When his eyes reopen, I silently push my plate his way. He grabs the sugar and pours it on top.

It used to seem like some sort of weird quirk that Jax would add sugar to everything—even a can of soda. I thought he maybe had a thyroid problem or something. His eating habits made so much more sense to me after I found he was fae—a supe species famous for having a sweet tooth.

But that doesn't make it any less disgusting to watch him eat.

It might even counterbalance those shoulder blades.

"Unicorn meat, my gods," Jax says. "I can't believe Oberon came through."

"Oberon," I say, recognizing the name Nico mentioned last night. "Jax, did you have something to do with the new client who visited my office last night?"

He preens, not noticing the WTF in my tone. "I might've recommended your services to a new associate of mine. And I might've also suggested Kirkland throw in a little something extra to sweeten the deal. Told him my girl's the best, and if you want the best, ya gotta be willing to pay for it."

Darron turns to me, one eyebrow raised. "I didn't realize you were a prostitute."

I slam my coffee mug down. "I am not—you know what? Never mind. Why am I even talking to you? And you—" I level my gaze at Jax, venom rising in my tone. "Don't bother boosting my business if you're only in it for some unicorn meat. Sweeten the deal?" I repeat his words, sarcasm dripping from my tongue.

"It's not like I should expect anything better," I add. "As usual, you're only in it to play an angle and get what you want. Meanwhile, you can tell yourself you're a good person because you threw some work my way."

He winks at me. "You're welcome. And I'm not a person, remember. I'm fae."

"Like I could forget," I snap, tossing my mug into the sink so roughly that it breaks.

"That's my cue to exit stage left, I believe," Darron says standing. "I'll start bringing in my things. My bedroom is in the back?"

"Hold up a minute," I interject. Pointing a finger at

Darron's chest, I demand, "What are you?"

He doesn't hesitate. "Human. One hundred percent. I have the DNA testing to prove it. Bit disappointing, to be honest. I was rather hoping for some small trace of something interesting. But..." He shrugs. "We can't all be supes, can we?"

Jax's arm comes around me, pulling me in close. On his other side he does the same to Darron. "Look at you two, bonding already!"

With two fingers Darron picks up Jax's arm and then quickly ducks away. I'm much less delicate. I put my elbow between Jax's ribs hard enough that he winces and stumbles away.

"My room?" Darron asks again.

"Yes, you can't miss it," Jax says, rubbing at the sore spot on his chest. "Lots of closet space. Your lady friend will love it!"

Now there's a woman too. Great.

My phone vibrates in my pocket with a reminder. I'm supposed to be at the job site at ten.

Now that I know who I have to thank for it, I'm not in any rush. "What kind of mess are you trying to pull me into?" I demand of Jax.

His eyes open wide, wounded and sad. "Babe..."

"Nuh-uh." I shake my head. "I'm not *your* girl or babe or anything else."

He sighs heavily, like a dog that's been scolded and is wondering how long it'll take to snuffle its way back into your good graces. "You know, fae marry for life."

"I didn't know you were fae when we got married," I remind him. "And neither did you."

The truth is, I did sorta suspect he was an asshole when we got married, so I can't say I went into it totally blind. But

I figured he'd grow out of it. For our wedding toast my dad said, "We'll see what happens between these two crazy kids, but in the meantime, this has been a hell of a party!" I guess everyone saw the writing on the wall. And yet, two years into our marriage, when I walked in on Jax having sex with another woman—I was shocked.

Okay, partially the shock was that they weren't *on* our bed, but above it. Both Jax and the girl had wings and were fucking mid-air. To this day he acts like it's a point of pride that he didn't defile our marriage bed.

That's how I found out my husband was fae. And a cheater. They both came as such a shock that to this day I don't know which I'm more angry about.

"Paige." He gives me the deep soulful look that worked on me for longer than it should've. "No matter how many times you stomp on my heart, it will always be yours." He reaches out with his delicate long-fingered hand and cups the side of my face. "Always."

I slap his hand away. "Get out, Jax."

He stands abruptly, a flash of anger crossing his face. "How many times do I have to apologize before you forgive me?"

"Just take these unicorn steaks," I shove them at him, "And leave."

"I can't. I have to help Darron move in. I promised, and you know a fae promise can't be broken."

"Too bad wedding vows don't count," I say crossing my arms.

"Do you think it's easy living between two worlds?" Jax asks, his volume rising as Darron comes up behind him, carrying a pile of red velvet pillows.

"Excuse me," he says politely edging past my ex, who is still ranting.

"Did I ask to be switched with a human baby at birth? To be raised away from Faerieland with no knowledge of my true origins? I repeat, Paige—I did not know I was fae!"

"But you did know that your dick could fit inside one," I say acidly.

He ignores me. He's on a roll now. "Now I'm a stranger in Faerieland and an outcast in the human world." Clenching his fists, he places them on his chest. "I am a castaway." He slumps dramatically and then stays in this position almost as if waiting for applause.

Or for me to gather him up in a big hug.

Instead I stand and head for the stairs. "Stay out of the attic," I yell in Darron's direction as he weaves his way back through the kitchen. "You might have a decade of free living in front of you, but I'll cut that short if I hear you outside my door."

"Oh, honey." He spins on his heel. "You're not my type. I prefer a more mature woman."

"Good call, man," Jax says, giving him a fist bump. "You'll live longer. But with Paige you'd die happy," he adds. "I have never found another girl, human or fae, that can give he—"

"OUT!" I scream at Jax, loud enough to scare his wings out. They pulse between his shoulder blades, gossamer fine, colored like a monarch. It just pisses me off more. Stupid shoulder blades. Stupid hot body. Stupid wings and even stupider face.

"GET OUT!" I yell again, and Jax goes, bumping into Darron who is now carrying in a full body mannequin.

What the fuck is even going on? My phone goes off again —my last warning that it's time to leave for work.

I don't have time to decide if I want to Kill, Marry (again) or Fuck Jax.

I have to go get down and dirty.

5

———

I stop to grab some coffee first, even though I already had one at home. I swear the aftertaste of those nasty cotton candy steaks stuck to the rim of my mug. I'm going to have to throw it out. That and everything Jax touched.

I need to retool my daily life, make sure that I'm focusing on Brent and our future together. He asked me to move in with him a few weeks ago and I told him...I needed to think about it. Then I started babbling about the house and how much it means to me. But Brent can only see the house as where I lived with Jax. And something that still connects me to him. He's not wrong about that.

We ended up having a whole "where is this relationship going" type fight... and I may have dropped a wheedling suspicion I have about his oh-so-gorgeous aide, Giselle. Like her famous namesake she looks like a model. Her red hair and puffy lips are the only part of her that's generously sized, the rest of her body is all angles. She's so skinny a stiff breeze could knock her over. When I stand next to her my own ample curves seem obscene in comparison. He says that I'm stuck in the past, and maybe not entirely over Jax. I said that I wasn't sure about his vision of the future where he's the ambitious politician and I'm the perfect smiling wife at his side, pretending like there's not a beautiful woman ten years younger than me clocking twelve hours a day at his side.

The fight ended with us deciding to take a break and think things over.

Which brings me here. A woman who no longer fucks her ex, but can still get fucked over by him.

Brent's right. Maybe it is time to let go of the house. And Jax too. And if I'm being honest, Brent has never given me any reason to suspect Giselle is anything more than his aide. Is she hot? Yeah. Is that his fault? No. I mean shit, it's not even her fault, really. Although, it's clear to anyone with eyes that she worships him. If he asked Giselle to bring him a virgin sacrifice, she'd whip her ever ready pen and paper from her bag and ask him, "Preferences on hair color, age, or size?" So yeah, Giselle is a little obsessed, but I'm not in a relationship with her.

It's time for me to grow up and put in that effort with Brent, not keep wistfully remembering the tidal wave of passion that was Jax. Trying to get your ex out of your life when he's also your landlord is extraordinarily difficult. But I can do that. It's time for Paige Harper to grow up.

Coffee in hand, I check in at the office, trying to ignore the candy-apple red Ferrari outside Nico's workplace.

It belongs to a wealthy woman who seems to make a living by getting married and divorced, then taking the man for everything she can. Normally, I'd say that's despicable behavior, but—given my morning—I almost wonder if I should cozy up to her and ask for some tips so that my next divorce is a little more financially lucrative.

I feed Vee crickets, as I'm out of the white mice she prefers. I figure she can earn her keep around here and actually catch some critters rather than living high on the hog. She actually turns her head when I present her with the bugs, but I've seen this behavior before.

"Won't do you any good, Vee," I tell her. "Although maybe we can work something out. You let me know any time a customer is a supe, and I'll add some mammal protein to your diet. Consider it a quid pro grow."

She cocks her gargantuan head like maybe she's listening, and before I can turn around, the crickets are gone.

"Or maybe you don't want to out the supes because they sent you here as a plant," I add. Vee makes a low gagging noise and I don't think it's in reaction to her diet. "Yeah, that was yet another pun," I tell Vee. "And if you want to plant roots here, you better get used to it." I realize I'm wagging a finger in the plant's face, as if it's a person. It occurs to me that maybe I need more friends. Or fewer plants.

A low moan comes from next door. Sounds like Nico is servicing Ms. Red Ferrari very thoroughly. I should do her a favor and just let her know that he's paid by the hour. She doesn't have to go through the whole rigamarole of getting married, hiring Nico to bust the new hubby for cheating, then have revenge sex with her private eye. She can skip all that and just go straight to the banging if she wants to save time.

Another moan followed by a squeal, and I can't help but remember Jax's shoulder blades and how lonely my attic bedroom can get. I wonder if werewolves ever go for missionary or if it's all strictly doggy style?

Okay, it's time to go. I'm wondering what Nico's preferred sexual positions are, so I've officially spent too much time listening to him through the wall. I'll have to let him know that he'll need to change his title from "private dick" to "public dick" unless he wants to invest in some insulation.

I glance at my phone. It's 10:30. The fae who hired me last night, Kirkland, told me to be at the house at ten sharp, so naturally I'm going to fuck with him a little bit. I'll get there when I get there, and he'll still pay me double.

From next door, another moan, low and guttural. That one must be Nico…

My mouth goes dry.

And now it's time to leave. Like really go. Like now.

My phone goes off as I'm getting into Vanna. It's Jax calling. Jesus, what now? Did he auction my virginity off to the highest bidder? I bet he'd offer to split the proceeds with me 60/40 (the bigger take being his, of course) and all I gotta do is lie there and pop a fake blood bag when it's over.

I don't answer. As I toss the phone onto the passenger seat it goes off again. I ignore it, even as it continues insistently vibrating as I head to the address the fae gave me last night.

After parking in front of the house, I reach for the phone.

"Seriously?" I ask. I have six missed calls. All of them Jax.

I really need to change the pic I have of him in my phone. It automatically transfers with all my settings when I upgrade and I keep meaning to change it, but always forget. He's super hot in the pic, and apparently I never got rid of the flying hearts effect. Red pulsing hearts rush across my screen when he calls yet again.

Dammit, I need to change it to something different. Maybe like a poison emoji, or one of those pimple popping videos. If I condition myself to associate gross things with Jax, maybe I'll find him gross, too. Eventually.

Jax must realize I'm not going to answer his call, so he switches to texts instead.

I know this routine all too well. This is the part where he realizes he has really and truly pissed me off. Now he will spend the next week demanding to know "How can I fix it?" He has never been able to fully grasp that some things once broken, just can't be fixed.

Early in our marriage I tried to get this concept across by throwing an entire set of dinner plates at him. This was in response to him borrowing several thousand dollars from my dad with the explanation that I had some 'female troubles' and needed a medical procedure. Dad gave it without question and never said a word about it to me. I'm sure Jax was counting on that when he took the money and gambled it away. What he didn't consider was that unlike him, my parents didn't keep secrets. The jig was up when my mom called in a panic. "Don't let those doctors take out your baby maker! I don't care what they say!"

I was furious when I realized what had happened. Thus the plate throwing. Jax, in apology, glued them back together. They were a mess, but he presented them to me with such pride.

That was also the day Jax and I visited the ER because his hand was accidentally super glued to my left boob. Turns out he got glue everywhere while putting those plates back together, and well... It definitely cut our makeup sex short. Even now, my mouth curls into a smile, remembering the look on the receptionist's face as we approached the triage center like the world's worst three-legged race team, except it was our arms that were the problem. Somehow I can't imagine Brent will ever end up with his hand super glued to my tits.

And I need to start looking at that as a *positive*.

The point is that Jax will be all up in my business for the next few days hoping that we can kiss and make up. But that's not happening. I ignore his text, tucking my phone into my pocket as I get out of Vanna.

There are no other cars in the drive, which is kind of weird. Kirkland said he would meet me here. Maybe his goodwill from last night evaporated with my lateness. But the front door is unlocked, so that's good enough for me. I waltz in like I own the place, not like I'm just here to clean it.

And man, does it need a cleaning. There's even dust on the dust. I run my finger over the dining room table and my finger comes away with a bunny trail. But underneath that, it's a very nice table. Most of the furniture is covered with drop cloths, so I shouldn't have to do much upholstery work, but this place is going to be a gold mine for me, if the fae is paying double.

I decide to check the upstairs and get a feel for the damage before going back out to the van for supplies. There's a beautiful old staircase that might actually be a joy to clean—

yeah, I can get geeky about my job, and I spin a story in my head as I head up to the second floor. Jay Gatsby could have lived here. I sigh to myself, knowing that such an observation would be totally lost on Jax.

Brent would get it. I can't help but feel a little wistful at the thought.

There it is, the reason why my current boyfriend can trump my ex, any day. He actually gets my literature references and even drops a few of his own. Yesterday we'd exchanged a series of texts about the merits of Steinbeck, and even though it was the most we'd talked in over a month, it had been weirdly hot. Like in a brainy way. It made me miss him, miss the way he actually seemed to think about things before just blurting them, how he looked at *me* during sex...and not just my tits.

I'm so lost in my thoughts that I don't notice the liquid dripping down the stairs until I step in it. It's deep, richly red...and there's so much! As I watch, another rivulet trickles alongside the first, spilling from the room at the top of the stairs. It's running out from under the door, and puddled in the hallway.

Did the fae guy hire a painter? I mean, what else could this be? Sure it looks like blood, but nothing bleeds this much. Still, I can't help but hesitate outside the door, wary of what I'll find on the other side.

With a shake of my head, I push that thought away. I cleaned the bathrooms last year after the Fiberama Food Fest. It was not pretty, but I survived. The worst I'm likely to find here is a big spill and a frustrated hired hand. I push open the door.

A gasp escapes me.

It turns out there's something worse than the natural end of a Fiberama Fest.

Because the spill is definitely not paint. It's blood. And a body lies on the floor.

But that's not even the most surprising find.

Standing over the body, holding a knife, is Jax.

6

"What the actual fuck?" I manage as I stare at Jax. My mouth hangs open as arterial blood sprays across his chest from the still-bubbling corpse on the floor.

"Paige!" Jax cries, dropping the knife. "You're okay!"

"Yeah," I say, backing up until I hit a wall. I pull the gun from my waistband, but I can't bring myself to point it at him so it hangs limply at my side. The blood is still running from the body, the pool pushing me further and further away. Not that I want to get close.

"I'm okay, but he is not. H-h-he's... he's dead," I stutter. "What did you do?"

"Me?" It's his turn to look surprised, and apparently— offended. "I did *not* do this, Paige."

"Okay," I take a deep breath. "I just found you standing over the body holding a knife, Jax. I mean, you've been caught literally red-handed. What did this guy do?" My eyes narrow and my stomach is revolting, sick at the thought I just had. The one, sickly-sugary bite of unicorn meat begins to make a journey back up my throat, but I hold it in. "Did you owe this guy money?"

"No! No, no, no, no..." Jax starts to wipe his hands on his jeans, but there's so much blood still spraying from this guy's neck that the denim is soaked through. "You've got to believe me! I got a call from Kirkland. He said you got hurt here at the house, and that I needed to come right away. I saw the blood under the door and..."

He closes his eyes, and damn if that cheating, lying, *murdering* son of a bitch isn't crying. "Oh God, Paige. I thought you were dead."

My heart squeezes a little at the sight of tears dripping down his perfect cheekbones. Laughing, joking, and kissing are his usual MO for getting out of a tight spot. He's never resorted to turning on the waterworks before.

But then I remember all the times he lied to me. There's too many of them to count. I harden my heart. "Save it for the cops," I say, pulling out my phone, gun still in my other hand.

"No, wait—listen!" Jax says, hands out, begging. "He was still alive when I got here, the knife was in his neck and I pulled it out...I was trying to help...I was trying—"

Jax actually lunges for me, and for the first time in my life, I'm truly scared of him. I dart away, but blood is covering the entire surface area of the floor. I go down, palms first, sliding through eerily warm blood. Both my gun and my phone are thrown across the room, but it's the phone I go for as I kick at Jax, scissoring my legs.

"Stay away from me!" I shout, while dialing 911, my thumb leaving a bloody print on the screen. A cool, calm voice answers.

"What is your emergency?"

"I'd like to report a..." I look at up at Jax, and he tries one last time, mouthing the word *please*.

Nope, sorry, buddy. One too many lies. One too many bait and switches. One too many women in his bed. He's let me down so many times. I can't trust him, and I'm lying in a puddle of proof.

"I'd like to report a murder," I finish, then rattle off my name and the street address. "I fell. In the blood," I tell them. Despite myself I start to cry.

"Shit, shit, shit," Jax says, raking his fingers through his hair—the only spot on him that didn't already have blood on it. "Fuck! You really did it."

"I did," I say, covering the phone with my hand. "I had to."

I hear the operator's voice yelling, "Ma'am? Ma'am, are you alone? Are you safe?"

"I'm going to tell them who you are and what I saw," I say, my voice thick with tears. Jax stares back at me looking frail and scared and all too human. For the first time since I've known him Jax might actually be feeling regret for something that he's done.

"Why did you call the cops?" he asks.

"Unbelievable," I shake my head. "Is anything ever your fault?"

His eyes are wide and locked on me. Jax gulps and then asks in a low voice, "That's a hypothetical question, right?"

I laugh, the sound both bitter and sad. From outside comes the distant wail of sirens.

And with that, my ex-husband—liar, cheater, thief, con-man, and now a killer—runs out of the house.

And hopefully, out of my life.

———

"So, your husband is a faery?" the cop, who had introduced himself as Detective McGinnis, asks.

"Ex-husband," I say, for the millionth time. "And I didn't know he was fae when I married him." I'm sitting on one of the downstairs couches, the drop cloth pulled around me for warmth. "He's a pixie, by the way."

"Thought he was a faery?" McGinnis says.

"Pixie is a type of faery. Fae. Just, listen..." I repeat Jax's name, physical description, and where he lives. "Seriously, he's not going to be hard to catch," I tell the cop interviewing me. "He's covered head to toe in blood."

His partner, Detective Sloane, comes into the front room, holding out his phone. "You're not kidding," he says. "Look what just came in."

He holds it out so we can both watch a YouTube video posted fifteen minutes ago. I watch as a blood-covered Jax is thrown to the ground, his cheek grinding against gravel as a knee goes into his back. He cries out in pain, and it would be heart-wrenching if not for the blinking neon sign I see behind him.

"You went to a strip club?" I shout.

"Wait!" he cries out in the video. "I just paid for a lap dance!"

I turn away from the video, not wanting to see anymore. But there's no way to keep my ears from hearing Jax's parting line, "Being horny isn't a crime!"

Whatever. What the fuck ever. Why can't being divorced mean that you're actually done with someone? Legally. Socially. Mentally. Emotionally.

Detective Sloane chuckles and walks away, calling to another cop waiting out by his car, "Hey, you gotta see this!"

"And you were here because?" McGinnis is holding a

notepad and still asking questions. I try to concentrate, try to think about something other than Jax.

"I was hired to clean," I explain.

"By who?"

"Whom," I correct, and he glances up. "I have to use my English degree when I can," I explain.

McGinnis nods, like this makes sense. "Yeah, my wife's got one of those."

"What does she do?" I ask.

"She works at a tire store."

I return the nod, because that also makes sense.

"I was hired by a guy named Kirkland. A fae, actually."

McGinnis makes a note. "And what's his last name?"

"I don't know," I admit, knowing it sounds super shady.

"Do you typically take work from strangers?" he asks.

"No," I snipe back. "I keep it to only friends and family, and don't charge them. It's a very lucrative business model."

"Do you typically take work from people whose names you don't know?" He tries again, patient despite my sarcasm. He reminds me a bit of my dad actually. I'd guess he's about the same age, probably getting real close to retirement judging by the amount of salt and pepper in his hair.

"No," I admit, tipping my head back onto the couch. "But my ex had recommended me to him as a cleaner and…" I shrug.

"The ex that just killed a guy?"

"Yeah," I mutter. "That ex."

Sloane comes back in and points a finger at me. "I know you. You're the hot cartoon girl with the mop." His eyes narrow as he sorta squints at me. "Maybe you look better when you're not all covered in blood."

"I know that place!" McGinnis says. "It's next to that werewolf P.I. my ex used when she thought I was running around on her. He tailed me for a solid month and I had no idea until I saw the pics."

I wrinkle my nose at this, having no sympathy for cheaters. "He sniffed out your secret love nest?"

"Ha! Yeah right." Sloane laughs and claps partner on the back. "All he discovered was that our friend here works too much and eats double cheeseburgers like they're going out of style."

"Yeah, now the wife has me on a vegan diet. It's killing me faster than any cheeseburger could," McGinnis explains mournfully, and I can't help but like him despite myself.

"Anyway..." He returns to his legal pad, although his face is a little red at this point. "You were hired to clean this house, showed up, found your ex-husband standing over a dead body—"

"First the blood," I correct. "So. Much. Blood. I didn't know a person had that much blood in them."

"They don't," Sloane comes back to the doorway. "The vic was a vampire."

"Really?" I ask, my eyes going wide. "Well...that explains it,"

"We got a serial killer pumping vamps full of blood thinners." He goes on. "One poke and SPEW! It's like every sip of blood they ever took comes pouring out of 'em."

I wince at this description. Even though I hate supes, I still get a tug of empathy. That guy upstairs was somebody's son, brother, or even ex-husband. He didn't deserve to get poked and go SPEW!

"Woah, woah, woah," I say. "You guys don't think Jax is... a serial killer? The guy that you're looking for?"

"Eh..." Sloane pulls a face. "Doubt it. That guy is good. Doesn't get caught. It's a messy crime scene, but not a messy criminal. He wouldn't be wandering around covered in blood, if you get my meaning."

"Your *meaning* being the literal fact that Jax was wandering around covered in blood, right?" I ask, biting back again. "So not like an inference or a subtlety?"

McGinnis shakes his head, flips his notebook shut. "English majors," he says under his breath.

"It's a messy way to go," Sloane says, ignoring my snipe.

At least this topic is more in my zone. "Who cleans it up?" I ask.

"That's a great question," McGinnis stands up, holding out a hand to me. I take it, and come to my feet, little black dots dancing across my vision. "Our usual clean-up crew got fed up and quit last week when we called them in for an assault case. Some sort of underground supe fight club. They were picking teeth out of cement."

"Ugh," I say, hands automatically going to cover my mouth.

"Seeing's how you were here to clean in the first place, and I doubt your mystery client is going to pay up...you want a job, Paige Harper?"

I look at the steps, at the blood that is starting to go cool and tacky. I straighten my shoulders, and will some steel into my spine.

"Will you pay me double?"

7

Of course they wouldn't. But I took the job anyway.

A girl's gotta eat. And pay rent. And clean up after her ex-husband's murders. At least the van is paid off. I go out to Vanna and wait for the cops to finish photographing the scene.

The coroner comes to remove the body, and I wonder whether his van is refrigerated or not, and if my cleaning supplies might be more effective if stored at a constant temperature. That's when I realize I'm probably in shock.

I haven't had a cigarette in years, but I bum one off a cop and smoke slowly, to calm my nerves. He gives me a once over that has nothing to do with sex.

"Wanna clean yourself up?" he asks.

I look down at myself, at the streaks of drying blood on my jeans and smears where I tried to wipe my hands on them. At least it's not fish scales. I send twin streams of smoke out of my nose.

"I've looked worse," I tell him and he leaves me with a nod. I did clean and stash my gun right away before they showed up...no need to muddy the waters any more than they already are.

I let out a long puff of smoke. A woman walks by, her dog sniffing at my bloody shoes. "What happened?" she asks.

"Vampire murdered," I tell her. She backs away, horrified.

"But...we're a Humans First neighborhood," she tells me "No supes allowed."

"Don't worry, there aren't any here now," I say, watching as the coroner's van pulls away. From the porch, the cop gives me the signal that it's my time to shine—literally. I take one last puff, flick the cigarette butt, and tell the woman, "Be sure to lock your windows and doors."

Back inside, all my shock is gone. Work can do that for me, the simple steps of making a mess go away helps put my mind in order, too. I make a mental list, and start checking boxes. With the things that I clean up, you gotta have an iron disposition and nerves of steel. I get to work with my wet vac, sucking up all the blood like a hungry vampire. I wince at the mental image and decide to pretend that the blood is cherry Jell-O that didn't set right. There's so much bloo—er, Jell-O—that I have to empty the tank container three times.

I'm on my hands and knees trying to get in between the floorboards, and lost in thought about how I really want another cigarette and how I shouldn't have had the one I did when a mosquito dive bombs my head. I slap at it with my rag, and there's a solid thump and a high-pitched voice squeaks, "*Fucking bitch!*" as something rolls across the floor.

Oh shit.

"Shauna?" I ask even as I silently pray, *Please don't let it be her.*

My ex-husband's annoying sister. We've only met a handful of times, but she always leaves a distinct impression. That's a pun. The first time we met, she slammed into my wall and I can still see her tiny outline in the drywall.

There's a loud pop and before me stands the pixie herself. She's petite, five foot nothing, less than a hundred pounds soaking wet. But she's not diminutive. Her bright pink hair is an indication of her bombastic personality. I used to tell Jax that she's a five-minute person. Like, I can be around her for five minutes before I seriously consider murdering her.

Shauna stares at me, her pupils dilated, probably high as shit. "Paige?"

I nod. Even though Shauna is Jax's sister, they didn't grow up together. Jax is a changeling, so he didn't even know his bio family until he was in his twenties. Shauna wasn't in his life when we were married, and I think she's barely been in it since we got divorced.

"Are you here because of Jax's arrest?" I ask, confused.

"Jax...got arrested?" She shakes her head then rolls her eyes "Figures. But no, I'm looking for Kit."

I take off my cleaning gloves and rub my face. Shauna has always been kind of wild, but then her wife disappeared during the ghosting. Since then she's gone full on dumpster fire. From what I heard she was heavy into drugs—or what pixies use as drugs.

"Where did you come from?" I ask. "A fashion show? A casting call?"

"A beauty pageant," she admits. Pixies get high off of beauty. Just one touch and they can steal a person's allure. Usually that person feels a little rough and looks a bit run down for a while. For the pixie though, it's like a hit of heroin.

"Okay, let's get you home. Where are you staying?" I ask, more than a little annoyed that I have to stop working on mopping up one of Jax's literal problems to figuratively mop up another.

But Shauna is staring at the pool of blood. "Whose is that?" she asks.

"I don't know, some vamp." I take her shoulders. "Why don't we go outside?" But she won't budge. Fine. We'll do this the hard way. "I'm going to tell you something that will be hard to hear," I say. "Jax killed someone here."

She shakes her head and says, "No. Jax wouldn't do that. I mean, I know he wasn't an awesome husband and that he can be a shit brother, but he's not a killer."

"I'm sorry, but I saw him standing over the body." I motion at the floor. "And it looked like the Overlook Hotel in here. I've been cleaning for hours."

Shauna crosses her arms against her chest, a gesture I know well from my ex. This is the 'I'm not listening to you' pose.

"I knew my brother was into something shady. I put an app on his phone so I could follow him." Her eyes land on the wall I haven't gotten to yet. Where sprays of arterial blood are drying. "Looks like I was too late."

"Too late to stop him from killing someone," I agree, tossing my sponge into the mop bucket. Red-tinged water laps over the sides. "But you're not too late to help me out with the walls."

"Not Jax," she says, shaking her head. "I'm talking about Kit. I put an app on *Kit's* phone."

I close my eyes, trying to remember the family details. To humans, supe families can get tricky fast. "Kit is your changeling brother, right? The one you were raised with, but was actually human, the one who was switched out with Jax as a baby?"

"Yes," Shauna nods, weirdly proud of me. "My *real* brother. He's a human who became a vampire. "

I'm about to correct her that her *real* brother by blood would technically be Jax, my ex, but I decide against it. Fae can be touchy about what constitutes family, and the fact that Kit had been turned into a vampire was kind of a sore spot.

"Okay," I say, walking myself through it. "But you're not looking for Jax, you tracked Kit here—" My eyes go to the wall and the red spray on either side of Shauna, dark and menacing when viewed through her pale, gossamer wings. "Oh shit," I say, understanding. There is some soap opera level of family drama going on here. "Um, Shauna...what does Kit look like?"

"Why?" she asks, then turns to see what I'm staring at. The long lines of dripping blood must make it clear to her as well, because she lets out a wail and collapses into a sobbing mess on the floor.

"Maybe it wasn't him," I try out while patting her on the shoulder, it's tiny under my hand, her bones like a little bird's. "Maybe he was hanging out with some vampire friends—"

"He didn't have friends!" Shauna wails. Her whole body shakes and I try to think of anything I can do for her. Anything to make it better.

"Look, I've got some sugar packets from my coffee," I tell her. "Do you want some sugar?"

She sniffles and nods.

"Okay," I help her up. "Maybe you can rest in the van while I...finish." She doesn't say anything as I lead her to Vanna and make a bed out of drop cloths and clean rags.

The door slides open for her and Vanna blinks her lights, almost in greeting.

"I think I know your van," Shauna tells me as she closes her eyes and drifts off to sleep. She must have fed off every one of those beauty contestants because she is out like a light, crashing hard even after the six sugar packets she ate —which included the paper because she's not exactly a patient pixie.

I shake my head and let out a long breath.

What the hell am I going to do with a cracked out pixie vamp?

———

After a few hours I have the house looking spic and span. Blood is hard to get out, but I'm a professional and I know my business.

I try to wake Shauna up, but she's snoring away, cuddled up between the bleach bottles and the mops. Sleeping off her bender.

I sigh. I'll bring her home tonight, but then I'm kicking her crazy pixie ass to the curb. She mutters in her sleep and guilt fills me. Her bio brother murdered her adoptive brother, I can't blame her for wanting to escape from reality for awhile.

I shake my head. Nope. This is not my problem. I will not be pulled into Jax's bullshit again.

I slam the door and Vanna gives me a little honk. "Sorry, girl," I say.

When we get to the house, I again try to wake up Shauna, but she's dead to the world. I pick her up like a baby—she's so light—and carry her inside.

"Who is our guest?" someone asks and I nearly jump out

of my skin. Shit. I forgot that Darron was here, lives here now. I've been on my own for almost ten years, and all of a sudden I have a full house. Well, one person feels full to me. One person plus a pixie is overload.

"Jax's sister," I tell him as I bring her up the stairs to the master bedroom that Jax and I used to share. I place her on the bed. Darron hovers at my side.

"Fae junky?" he asks and I give him a look.

"Honey, I may be older, but that just means I've seen more of the world." He turns on one heel gracefully. "I'll make us some coffee. That girl is going to be sleeping for a while."

I follow him out, "And you know that because?"

"Fae don't overdose the way we do. She'll just sleep it off and have beautiful dreams," he tells me.

"Are you a...supe doctor?" I ask, not impressed at the idea. Great. Now we'll have house calls. Harpies with shredded wings and manticores with broken ankles showing up in the middle of the night.

He shakes his head. "No. I was a performer, though."

"An actor?"

"On the stage...there are always a lot of faerie folk in the arts."

"Is that how you know Jax?" I wouldn't be surprised at all if Jax had tried to break onto Broadway. He never realized his self-righteous monologues only sounded good to him.

Darron pours some coffee, asks how I like it. "Milk, no sugar," I tell him. I have a distaste for sweet coffee since breaking up with Jax.

"Sort of," Darron says, answering my question. "A fae friend of mine got me into a high stakes poker game."

"You're friends with supes?" I ask, wrinkling my nose. That's different than just working with them. If his profession of choice was invaded by fairies with flair, I get that. But choosing to spend off hours with supes is a different story.

Darron adds milk and sugar to his cup, then sits. "My wife always used to say, it takes all kinds."

"Yeah," I say, staring down into my tea. "All kinds. Faeries, ex-husbands, and murderers. It's just when they're all rolled into one that it gets to be a little much."

My mouth pulls down at the corners and I realize I'm going to cry, right here into my coffee, right in front of this stranger. I wipe madly at my eyes, but Darron reaches out and takes one of my hands.

"Girl, what is going on with you?"

An incredibly loud pixie snore tears through the second floor, and I let the tears fall. "How much time have you got?"

8

By this fourth cup of coffee Darron is about as jacked up as Shauna, who is still sawing logs upstairs. He repeats my story, hands shaking with the caffeine while I pull some hot pizza rolls out of the oven. In times of stress I always find that consuming junk food makes life a little less miserable.

"So, your ex-husband murdered his changeling brother, you saw it happen, and Shauna shows up to find out that her family just got smaller by one, and that her other brother has been arrested for murder?"

"I didn't exactly see it happen," I clarify. The cops had gone over the story with me repeatedly. "I just saw Jax standing over Kit with a knife."

"Poor girl," Darron says, shaking his head.

"I'll be alright," I say, leaning forward to press my palms into my eyes.

"I mean Shauna," he tells me, and I push back from the table. "Don't get excited," he says, gesturing for me to stay. "You obviously *are* fine. You just cleaned up after a murder that's being pinned on your ex-husband and you aren't in the fetal position."

"Fetal position sounds kind of nice right now," I admit.

Darron is quiet for a second, watching me over the still-steaming pizza rolls that I set between us. "May I submit a theory?"

"Sure," I say. I'm not in the murder-solving business, I'm a cleaning lady. But if Darron wants to sound off—and I'd bet he's going to defend his buddy Jax—I'm willing to listen. As much as my ex has pissed me off over the years, I'd love a reason to believe I didn't marry a murderer.

"You can't kill a vampire with a knife," Darron tells me. "A least, not just a knife."

I stop and think. It's true. It's not easy to kill a vamp, and there are plenty of horrible videos from underground Humans Firsters to prove it. A stab to the neck wouldn't do it.

But I already know that more than a knife was involved. "The cops said that there's a vamp serial killer on the loose. Uses blood thinners so they bleed out fast."

Darron leans back in his chair, resting his tea cup on his knee cap. "Blood thinners. Interesting...I was in a production of *Hamlet* once where we ran out of stage blood."

"Cool, who were you playing?" I ask, genuinely interested. It's the Lit geek in me.

"Claudius," Darron says. "Hamlet's—"

"Uncle," I finish for him. "Great soliloquy."

"One of the best," Darron agrees, but looks confused.

"I was an English major," I explain. "Now, I'm a cleaning lady."

"Makes sense," he says, and I can't do anything other than agree.

"Anyway," Darron goes on. "Right before I'm to go on

stage we find out a confused baby vamp who'd been living in the orchestra pit—a story for another time—had raided our stage blood packs thinking they were real blood. The girl playing Ophelia was a vamp, so one of the stage hands just took a swipe at her arm."

"Like, just cut her?" I ask, shocked.

"It was a game we used to play," he says, a dreamy smile of days gone by playing across his lip. "We'd cut vamps and they'd bleed all over, magically close their own wounds, and we'd leave the mess for the matinee crew to find."

"That's...very theatre people of you," I say.

"But we didn't know Ophelia had been taking blood thinners," Darron says, suddenly serious again.

"On purpose?" I ask, confused.

Darron shrugs. "Humans don't have a monopoly on stupidity." He picks up a pizza roll and takes a dainty bite. "Hideous," he murmurs, setting it back down onto the plate.

Now it's my turn to shrug. "Just means more for me."

"Anyway," he continues, "She was going to a straw party after the performance. You know what those are?"

"Humans cut themselves and vamps walk around with straws, taking samples." It's kind of like Saturday afternoon at Costco but with Type O blood instead of Grade A meat. It's also an awesome way to spread diseases—diseases that vamps can't catch but humans can. Supes, always out for a good time and not worrying about who it hurts. "Speaking of stupidity, they can't be the brightest humans, slicing themselves up for vampires."

"Oh, I don't know about that," Darron laughs lightly. "There's a certain thrill in having a beautiful vamp inform you that your blood has a cherry hibiscus bouquet that ought to be bottled."

"You're a vamp groupie," I groan. Sitting up taller, I point a finger at him. "No vamp parties here. Ever. I don't care what deal you have with Jax, you'll be out of here."

Reaching across the table, Darron lays his hand over my pointed finger. "I am not a groupie. I am a student of life." My hand sinks to the table. Darron smiles. "You were so young when people realized supes walked amongst us. But me, I was middle-aged. Realizing I'd lived half my life with a mind so closed I wouldn't have believed supes existed if I hadn't seen them with my own eyes..." He shakes his head. "It shook me. Right down to my toes. And I decided from there on, I would live fully. Wide-eyed and open to all experiences."

For a second I'm envious of him. The supes came and was inspired. Where Darron opened up, I instead closed down. But then I remember all the supes have taken from me.

I bite into my next pizza roll a little more viciously than is necessary. "So finish your theater story. The blood thinner vamp."

"Ophelia, yes. She was thinning out the blood in her system so that she could intake more at the party, but the stage hand didn't know. He cut her, and...well..." Darron's enthusiasm fades as the story takes a bleak turn. "Let's just say it was a good night for her understudy."

"She died?"

Darron nods. "The emergency room staff wasn't exactly in a hurry to give her all the transfusions she needed to survive. There were a few Humans Firsters working that night, and more than a few medical workers don't believe the Hippocratic Oath covers supes."

I've heard that, but I'm not going to debate the point. Something much more important has my attention. "So you're saying what? That you think Kit dosed himself with the blood thinners? Like it was suicide?"

"No, what I'm saying is that the vamp serial killer could very well be another vampire. They know the drug. They're familiar with it."

"But Jax isn't a vampire," I say, and then add, "The cops seemed pretty certain Jax wasn't the serial killer. He was too sloppy."

"Excellent point," Darron agrees. "Also I should note that blood thinners take time to work. Jax left the house shortly after you did this morning."

I narrow my eyes, seeing where Darron is taking this. "Okay, fine. I get it. He had no motive. The timeline doesn't work and he can't even correctly cook a boxed cake mix, so it seems unlikely he could follow a serial killers blueprint well enough to accurately copycat him."

All I know is that supe families are insane. And Kit and Jax didn't exactly love each other. They were swapped out at birth and when Jax tried to go back to his fairy folk they jumped at the chance, basically disowned Kit. There's bad blood between those two," I tell Darron. "And I just finished cleaning it all up."

"Hmm..." Darron says, as if he's considering my point. "How convenient you were there though, am I right?"

"What do you mean?" I ask. "Of course I was there. I was hired—"

Oh shit. Yeah, I was hired by Kirkland, a random fae whose last name I never got, who wanted me to show up at a specific house at a specific time. When I did, I found my ex standing over a body...and never heard from my supposed employer after that. And what had Jax said, right before I called the cops? He said my employer had called him, claiming that I had been hurt on the job.

Someone wanted us both there at the same time.

Both there, standing over a body.

"What the fuck is going on?" I ask Darron.

"I don't know, dear," he says, sipping his tea. "But it sounds like you're right in the middle of it."

9

W ith all the coffee in my system it's impossible to fall asleep.

During those jittery sleepless pre-dawn hours I soothe my conscience by making the decision to visit Jax the next day. I'll tell him I'm sorry that I thought the worst of him, although let's be honest, it was a nice novelty for me to be in a room with Jax and not be thinking about touching him. I'd actually been repelled by him for a split second there. If I'd been more on my toes I would've snapped a pic to remind myself that...that what? Jax can commit actual murder practically right in front of me, and after one conversation I think he's likely innocent?

I shake my head, trying to clear it. Either he has royally fucked with my head enough that I can't imagine him being guilty, or he actually is innocent and someone very badly wants him to go down for it. Whichever way I cut it, one of us is fucked.

Tomorrow I'll ask him what really happened. I mean, yeah, he'd already sort of told me, but this time I plan on actually listening. Also this conversation will happen through a glass window and with guards watching so there's no chance of me throwing dishes or him getting superglued to my boobs.

Maybe I can also call those cops and tell them that I overreacted a little bit and on second thought, I'm pretty sure Jax didn't do it. But I kind of doubt you get a do-over on calling in a murder.

Maybe if I'm really lucky they'll have already figured out Jax clearly wandered into the wrong place at the wrong time and are even out looking for the real bad guy. Or maybe they already caught them!

But the odds of that seem pretty low. The cops were pretty eager to accept the murder as some sort of fae versus vamps thing and call it a day. Put another one in the books by hauling the guy holding the knife and covered in blood off to jail. Well, when I put it that way, it doesn't sound presumptuous so much as good detective work.

I finally drift off to sleep while imagining myself giving an impassioned speech to the jury that's deciding Jax's fate. Somewhere along the way, pretend melts into full on dreaming where I'm Jax's lawyer, but for some reason I'm wearing only my underwear. Despite being underdressed, I am witty and wise and persuasive. I'm like Matlock, but with a push up bra and a lacy thong instead of a three-piece suit.

My dream is interrupted by the creaking of the door that leads up to the roof. The one that opens up to the widow's walk. I always thought I was being practical—if mixed with romantic—about choosing the attic as my bedroom. Any home invader would have to know the layout of the house to come right for me, and I had an easy escape plan.

Now, though, hearing the door creak open it occurs to me that maybe I should put a lock on it. I'm sure the original owners never considered the possibility of winged supes breaking in, but I should have.

I reach for my gun...and it's not there. I left it downstairs earlier when I confronted Jax this morning. Still, the dark figure coming down the stairs doesn't know that.

"I've got a gun," I call out.

"I'll one up you," a laughing male voice responds. "I've got donuts."

"Brent!" I leap from my bed and reach him just as he gets to the bottom of the stairs and shove him hard enough that he stumbles. "You scared the hell out of me! How did you..." Seeing the coil of rope slung over his shoulder, I don't bother finishing the question.

Brent isn't just ex-military. He was a Navy SEAL. Climbing the side of my house is exactly the type of thing he likes to do. It proves he hasn't gone soft. That he's still "got it."

Brent is tall, lean, and ropey. There's not a bit of softness on him anywhere. As he grabs me and pulls me in close, the hardest part of him throbs against my belly. I'm still annoyed with him for scaring me, but that doesn't keep my hips from rubbing up against him.

"Mm, baby." His hands go up into my hair, gripping tight as we grind against each other like teenagers. "I couldn't stay away from you. I needed to see you tonight."

I start working at his belt, evidence of his sincerity eagerly waiting. *Eat your heart out, Giselle*, I think. Aloud, I say, "You couldn't use the front door?"

"I thought this would be a romantic gesture," he replies, tugging my shirt off over my head.

"What about the donuts? Just a ploy to keep you from shooting?" We're now very close to naked and I'm realizing how very much I've needed this. All the horny thoughts about Nico and Jax were just because I wasn't getting any. But that doesn't mean I won't shut this all down if he was bullshitting about the donuts. I strongly believe in making it clear which boundaries should never be crossed. Joking about donuts is one of them.

Luckily, Brent knows me better than that. "They're in my backpack," he assures me as he pushes me backwards onto the bed. "You want them?" He kneels between my legs and kisses the sensitive skin on my inner thighs. "Or do you want me?"

"You," I manage to gasp as his tongue finds my clit. "You."

———

B rent wears me out.

He's one of those super focused A-type personalities. Anything he does, he's gonna do it to the best of his ability. And then some.

The two of us have a lot of fun in bed. And yet...there are times when I feel like it could be even better if he let go a little and tried just a little bit less. The best sex with Jax was when we both lost our minds, but even when he comes Brent looks uber-focused, like he's firing missiles instead of blowing his load. He doesn't orgasm, he wargasms.

Still that's a dumb thing to complain about when he is so very generous in bed. He goes down on me like a man who lost his virginity to a succubus...which he did. Apparently, he found out when she friended him on Facebook. So we have 'unknowingly banged a supe' in common.

By the time Brent and I finish we are sweaty and worn out.

"You want your donut now?" he asks me.

"Too tired," I just manage to say as sleep washes over me. "Tomorrow. Morning."

That's the last thing I remember. The next thing I know, the sun is streaming through the windows and people are shouting downstairs.

"You crazy little pixie bitch, I'm going to have you and your friend arrested for trespassing!"

My eyes fly open and I sit up straight in bed as I recognize Brent's voice.

Shit. I grab my clothes from off the floor while straining to hear Shauna's reply. The buzz of her little voice is clear, but I can't quite make out the exact words. Still, I'm pretty sure it's not something conciliatory. That's not really Shauna's style.

I pound down the stairs. At the bottom, Shauna and Brent face off. Darron is nearby too, watching with arched eyebrows. I follow the direction of his gaze to the small neon green gun Brent has pointed at Shauna's midsection. Anyone else would think it was a toy. But I know exactly what it is because Brent tried to give me one just like it a few months ago.

It's a magic stun gun specifically designed to work on supes. Apparently they were popular back when any supes deemed dangerous were sent to a special prison in the underworld. They eventually shut that down after judges ruled it denied supes their basic human right of due process —carefully glossing over the fact that they aren't human. Laws were also passed making the magical stun guns illegal. But that doesn't mean that one can't be gotten on the black market.

I refused to take the gun. Not because it's illegal, but because I don't want to rely on something powered by magic. Give me old-fashioned gunpowder any day. But

Brent believes we need to take any advantage we can get. He got it from a rabid Humans Firster at a gun show, and even though the supes haven't given me any reason to love them —or even defend them—I was not happy with the fact that Brent had been in a shady transaction with a Firster. Those people are as loony as the supes.

Shauna seems to know exactly what it is too, although instead of trying to avoid getting temporarily stunned into a pile of senseless goo, she's egging Brent on.

"Go on, do it," she taunts. "I've got a hangover like you wouldn't believe, so you'd be doing me a favor. Spending a couple hours with no feeling in my body sounds pretty good right now."

"Brent, no," I interrupt, wedging myself in between him and Shauna. He immediately tips the gun down, but his gaze on me is not loving.

"Don't get in the middle of this, Paige," he warns.

"Um, hello, you're in *my* house," I remind him.

"Actually, it's Jax's house," Brent counters. "And you know I hate that you live—"

Shauna interrupts before he can say more. "Hey, about that," Shauna says from behind me. She taps at my shoulder insistently until I reluctantly turn to face her. "What am I doing here? The last thing I remember from yesterday was looking for Kit. Well, I hit the Miss Teen New Jersey pageant, then looked for Kit. Then I woke up here and I didn't even know where here *was* until I came downstairs and this nice gentleman"—Shauna indicates Darron— "was kind enough to fill me in."

Aw crap. Shauna doesn't remember finding me cleaning up Kit's blood. Or finding out that he died. Which means that I gotta tell her all over again. A pixie hangover can run anywhere from mild grumpiness to total amnesia, and I'm pretty sure Shauna was just about OD'd after tapping into several teen beauty queens. I'm going to have to ruin her world all over again.

"Happy to be of help," Darron murmurs before I can deliver the bad news. He tips an imaginary hat at Shauna then looks to me. "Do mornings here always begin with threats of violence? I could see that becoming tedious over time."

"He's the violent one!" Shauna screeches in her high-pitched voice. She points a little finger at Brent. "He walked in here like he owns the place, took one look at me, and told me I could walk out on my own two feet or he could carry me out in pieces."

Okay. I have to admit that does sound like a slight over-reaction to finding someone unexpected in the house. Actually, it sounds like a huge overreaction.

A quick glance at Brent, though, tells me he wouldn't agree with that assessment. Instead of looking embarrassed for going all commando before 9 am, he watches Shauna with all his concentration, like she might shrink to pixie size and try to kamikaze us all at any moment.

Pixies may look adorable when they shrink to their most pint-sized proportions. But this is actually when they're at their deadliest. My dad once got a job shoveling debris that was a house before a pissed off pixie plowed through it. I've heard they do something to manipulate the air around them, but really I don't need to understand the physics to be wary of them.

Still, I feel fairly confident that Shauna wouldn't mess with this house. She and Jax may not be super close, but she wouldn't destroy his property just for kicks. Honestly, Brent should give me a little more credit for having enough sense to know who is and isn't a threat in my own damn house.

Fury flows through me. As sudden as it is unmistakable.

Yesterday I woke to Jax taking over my house and this morning it's Brent. Different reasons, different methods—sure. But one thing is the same. Neither one took two damn seconds to ask me what I wanted. Neither one of them acts like my opinion matters at all.

Marching over to Brent, I snatch the gun out of his hand. Or at least, I try to. But he wasn't a SEAL for nothing. He dodges me smoothly and I end up climbing him like a monkey as I try to wrangle the gun away from him.

"Paige, what the hell?" he demands, flipping me over his back and setting me—unharmed—back on my own two feet. The ease with which he makes it perfectly clear that he can physically own me at any time makes me even more furious.

"This is my house!" I shout. Brent opens his mouth and I quickly add, "Don't you dare mention Jax again!"

"Jax," he snarls the name. "How can I not mention him when this *pixie*"—he says the word like it's a curse— "is only here because of him." Brent pulls a newspaper that he had folded and stuffed into his back pocket and holds it up in front of my face. "And when you're on the front page of the Wienerberg News because of him."

EX-WIFE FINGERS FAE HUSBAND IN BLOODY MURDER, the headline screams. Below that is Jax's mugshot and next to it is a photo of the front window of my storefront. Despite my horror at being in the paper, I can't help but also wonder if this might be good publicity for the business. 'I'm so good, I cleaned up after my husband's murder spree!'

Also, I really wish they hadn't said I *fingered* Jax. That probably didn't help matters with Brent.

Shauna shrinks to pixie size and lands on my shoulder. "I wanna see!"

Quickly, I push the paper down. "Shauna, there are donuts hidden somewhere in my bedroom. If you can find them—they're yours."

Brent makes a strangled sound, like he wants to say no, but realizes he has pushed me far enough. Also, like me, maybe he sees some value in getting Shauna out of our hair for a while.

"I'll help her," Darron volunteers, making me like him even more for being able to read the room. Gotta give theatre people credit. I mean, especially since most of them don't have jobs related to their craft. Us useless majors gotta stick together.

"Donuts, I'm coming, and I'm gonna eat every one of you little delicious bastards!" Shauna shouts, her wings flapping wildly as she flies up the stairs. Darron follows at a slower and more dignified pace.

Once they're gone, I turn back to Brent. "How do you know Shauna is related to Jax?" I demand.

He pauses and what might be doubt or even regret briefly crosses his face. But it's gone in an instant, replaced by his usual expression of stoic self-assurance. "I had a thorough background check performed when we started getting serious."

"When we started getting serious?" I repeat. "What does that even mean? Our first date or our first fuck?"

"I don't like this side of you," Brent says coolly.

"So, our first fuck then, huh?"

"Yes!" he snaps. "Why is that wrong? I liked you. I knew that I wanted to see more of you and I was fairly certain that you felt the same way. But I also needed to protect myself and my whole campaign team. We've worked too hard for it to be ruined by…" He holds out his phone screen with the horrible headline once again. "This type of trashy scandal."

Before I can answer Shauna's little voice screeches from above, "Wow, champagne too!" Followed by a loud, audible pop.

This gives me pause. "Champagne?" I question Brent.

His expression somehow grows even stonier. "Part of a little breakfast I prepared with mimosas, donuts, and…"

"Shauna, don't just suck the chocolate off the strawberries," comes Darron's voice from above.

I stare at Brent who looks back at me blandly. "Chocolate-covered strawberries too?"

He gives a half shrug in response.

"Seems like a kinda romantic breakfast," I observe.

"Does it?" he responds, still giving me nothing. And definitely not answering my silent question of what the special occasion is.

"It was pretty clear from last night you missed me. So the breakfast, is what? You trying to convince me to move in with you again?"

The rapid flapping of wings alerts me to Shauna's return. She zips between me and Brent. "Thanks for breakfast, you big doink. The donuts were good, the strawberries needed more sugar, champagne is gross, and this yellow gold monstrosity is trash—" With that she spits something at Brent's chest and then zooms away. The thing she spit bounces against him and hits the floor.

"I'm outta here," Shauna says, raising her two middle fingers in good-bye as she exits through an open window. Unfortunately, there's a screen on the window, so she leaves a pixie-sized hole behind.

"Great," I mutter, while Brent squats to pick up whatever

Shauna spit at him. I look down to see him pick up with two fingers a bright and shiny...

Ring.

"Oh shit," I say. "You weren't going to...propose?" I can't hide the look of horror on my face. If I'm not ready to move in with him I'm sure as shit not ready to get married. Not again.

Standing, Brent studies the ring. "I was going to, yes." His fist closes around the ring, hiding it from view. Then he shoves into his pocket. "What a mistake that would've been."

Turning on his heel, he heads toward the door. Open-mouthed I stare at him. I should let him go. I don't want this. I mean, I don't think I do. It's crazy to feel offended by him calling the very idea of it a mistake. But I *am* offended. No, it's more than that. I'm pissed off.

Because it feels like he's calling all of this—our whole relationship—a mistake.

He opens the door to reveal Giselle standing on the other side. Judging by the embarrassed look on her face, she has clearly overheard everything that has happened inside.

"What is she doing here?" I demand.

Brent doesn't even have the decency to look bad about having his aide hanging around. "Giselle came by this morning to bring me the newspaper."

"Wow, thanks for that, Giselle," I say sarcastically.

Her eyes narrow as they settle on me. "There's no waiting on damage control for this type of thing," she informs me in her throaty voice. Reaching out, she rubs Brent's arm in a proprietary way. "It's my job to watch out for him."

The dark cloud around him clears for a microsecond as he sends a smile of gratitude Giselle's way. "I don't know what I would do without you."

"Well, I do," I snap. "You'd be drinking champagne out of my belly button right now and I'd be eating a donut off your—"

Brent cuts me off. "I think we've both said enough for today."

Like hell we have.

No way am I gonna spend the rest of the day stewing. We're finishing this fight—right here and right now.

I grab the back of Brent's shirt, pulling him back into the house and then slam the door in Giselle's face.

"You don't get to be mad at me," I say. "I didn't do anything except live my life. And then you show up in the middle of the night with plans to propose and whatever else. But how the hell am I supposed to know that?"

Brent is frozen in front of me. He doesn't try to pull away, but he also stares pointedly away from me.

I sigh and then even though he's not looking at me, I point to the ceiling. "Darron, the guy who's probably drinking that champagne right now, is my new roommate. Jax brought him yesterday after he lost some sort of bet. I didn't like it, but...Darron's okay."

"I see," Brent says coldly.

"You need to see more," I say. "Like Shauna was here because she found out yesterday that her brother died. That's who Jax is accused of killing. And I didn't finger him, I mean, I did." I stop, shaking my head. "I thought Jax did it, but now I don't think he did, but I already told the cops he was guilty, so..."

Brent finally turns to face me. "You couldn't have mentioned any of this before?"

"When?" I demand. "You didn't really seem like you were in a mood for chatting last night."

"You could've found a time," he insists.

"Okay, sure," I say. "How about when you went down on me? From now on I'll take that as my cue to start filling you in on my day. For some silly reason I thought that starting a conversation with, 'So you know my ex-husband Jax? Well, he may or may not have murdered someone,' might put you off from sucking my clit." I say that last bit extra-loud so Giselle doesn't have to strain to hear.

Brent's eyes narrow. "Jax shouldn't be part of the conversation at all." He pushes his hand through his perfectly combed and styled hair, messing it up. It actually makes him look even sexier, but I know he'll be horrified the next time he looks in the mirror. Taking a step closer to me, Brent puts his hands on my shoulders. "Paige, this is your chance to finally distance yourself from him. Pack up your things. If you're not ready to move in with me, fine. We'll find you another place. But get out of here. You never have to see Jax again."

This is Brent bending, I realize. He's holding out an olive branch. I can meet him halfway and salvage our relationship.

Except I can't.

I always knew he was a bit of a control freak, but this morning I've seen a whole new side of him. And I'm not sure if I like it.

Or maybe it's because Jax probably didn't kill anyone and it's my fault he's sitting in jail. He didn't have enough sense to change his bloody clothes after fleeing the crime scene, and I can't see him making any decisions that will help him go free.

But the biggest maybe is the same one that kept me from putting a piece of lead in Jax yesterday. It's not his nice shoulders either. It's that he knew my parents. We spent tons of time with them as a couple and even later when we were divorced he'd still go to them. How many times did my dad say, "Jax, please stop calling me Pops. I didn't like it when you were married to Paige and I sure as hell can't stand it now that you're divorced." But Dad begrudgingly liked Jax, even when he hated him for the way Jax treated me. With my parents gone, Jax is one of my last links to them. More importantly, he talks about them as if they'll be back some day. I need that.

I take a deep breath and step back so that Brent's hands are no longer on my shoulders. "You should know. I'm going to visit Jax in jail today," I tell him. "I at least owe him that."

Brent's face hardens, his beautiful cheekbones becoming even more pronounced. "All right," he says as his hands fall to his sides. "It sounds like you have a busy day then. I won't keep you any longer."

This time when he walks out the door, I let him go.

10

It's amazingly easy to get in to see Jax.

He's in a jail designed for supes, and I get the distinct feeling that the guards are fairly lax when it comes to human visitors. I still have a passport from years ago with my married name, and since Jax hasn't been charged yet, we don't even have to talk behind one of those plexiglass walls you see on TV. I think if he had been arrested for killing a human, things would be very different, but none of the people in charge are going to lose sleep over a dead vamp.

I enter the visiting room full of spouses and children and loved ones and spot Jax at a corner table. I'm not allowed to touch him or hand him anything, but that's fine. All I want from him is answers.

"Paige!" Jax stands, then sits, then stands. "You've got to let me explain!"

"That's why I'm here," I tell him.

"I didn't murder Kit!" he tells me. "I was set up. You have to believe me!"

"I didn't at first, but I'm starting to," I admit. "They want to make it out that you're some kind of vamp serial killer."

Jax shakes his head. "They just want to pin those murders on someone, and if they can find a supe to take the blame, even better. But I've never killed anyone. Yes, I'm a cheater and a jerk and a trickster, but I am not a murderer." He has dark bags under his eyes.

"Are you okay in here?" I ask, wishing I didn't feel compassion toward him but unable to turn it off.

"Yeah. Hooked up with a bunch of biker fae. They love the shit out of pixies. They say I'm with them, so no one else will bother me."

"Watch out for the vamps," I tell him.

"You don't have to tell me twice. But they pretty much stick to their own. I'm keeping a low profile."

I stare at him, with his striking good looks and easy charm. He wouldn't know how to keep a low profile if his life depended on it. Which it might. But then again, this is a jail for supes. Everyone is hot. I mean, on a human scale I'm no slouch, but the guards didn't even give me a onceover when I came in here.

"I didn't hate Kit," Jax says. "I barely knew him."

"Then tell me what happened," I say. "I want to believe you, Jax. For the first time in your life, you're not digging yourself out of a hole with me." I narrow my eyes. "And this better be damn good."

"I set you up with that cleaning gig in good faith," Jax says "Kirkland needed a cleaner, and of course I thought of you. But then he told me you were at that house, hurt. So I rushed over and Kit was there on the ground gushing blood."

"The knife?" I ask.

"I pulled it out of his throat. I was just thinking I

wouldn't want a knife in *my* neck..." He puts his face in his hands. "It was stupid, but you know I'm not good with impulse control."

"Is that why you immediately went to a strip club?" I ask, not able to keep the bitterness out of my mouth.

Then he looks at me with his beautiful brown eyes and says, "I needed some comfort! And I didn't kill Kit."

"Then who did? And why would they frame you for it?" There are so many people that hate Jax. It could be anyone. Someone he cheated at cards, someone whose wife he slept with, someone who has an axe to grind with him being fae. The Humans First movement isn't above pinning crimes on supes, just to bolster their own arguments that they aren't to be trusted.

"I'm not sure who wanted me to go down for this," Jax says. "But I have a few ideas. It'll take some digging, and I don't know how safe it will be." He pauses and then leans forward. "Paige, when Kirkland told me you were hurt, I..." His eyes well up with tears and I have to look away before I start crying, too. The truth is, if someone told me that Jax was hurt or dying—I'd come running too. It doesn't matter that I stopped wearing his ring years ago. A part of me will always consider him family.

"I want out of here," he goes on. "But I don't want any harm to come to you because of me."

"Don't worry your pretty little head about mine," I tell him. "I know a P.I. who I can ask to look into it."

"Paige, you're my favorite!" Jax lights up like the Christmas tree we had on our first Christmas together. It was real, and Jax never watered it, and it caught on fire. Maybe I should be thinking more about those times and less about the gorgeous, tortured man in front of me. "You're the best," Jax says. "I never should have cheated on you..."

"But," I cut him off, before that line of thought goes too far. "I want something in return."

"Anything," he agrees. "You want to get back together? Done."

"No," I shake my head. "Definitely not that." I take a deep breath. "I want the house. Signed over to me. No tricks, no loopholes. The house is mine, free and clear."

Jax clenches his teeth and grimaces. "That might be a problem."

Of course it might. I should have been thinking about the burning Christmas tree after all, and taken it as the warning it was—both then, and now. A warning that Jax is a little boy who never grew up. Peter Pan with a bigger penis and an admitted impulse control problem.

"I wanted to buy into this big underground supe poker game," Jax says. "But I was a little light on cash."

"You didn't," I say. My teeth grind together and I get black dots in my vision, anger exploding inside of me. The guards already said we can't touch, but it's going to take more than Captain Pectorals over there to keep me from killing Jax with my bare hands if he says what I think he's going to say.

"I used the house as collateral."

Yep. There it is. I have to kill him now. I'm afraid if I open my mouth I'll breathe fire. "You are fucking kidding me."

"I know, I know. And after I made that deal with Darron. If I lose the house, what will become of him?"

"What. Will. Become. Of. *Darron*?" I repeat, barely able to get the words out past the ball of anger in my throat.

Jax's eyes widen at the look on my face and he tries to backpedal. "And you too. I'm worried about what would happen to you too."

"You should be worried about yourself, asshole," I say,

standing up to leave. My hands are shaking and I realize that I'm not just angry. I'm hurt too. Why do I let Jax do this to me every time? "You just lost your only supporter on the outside."

"Paige, no...wait!" He stands with me, and the guards move closer to our table, watching us closely. "I can fix this," he pleads, hands in front of him, almost in prayer. "Haven't I fixed everything before?"

"Not everything," I say tightly, but I do sit back down. "Remember Jacelyn?" That was the name of the fae girl I caught him with, floating six feet above our bed and delivering on all kinds of new positions from that height.

"Jacelyn?" Jax echoes, his eyes become unfocused and dreamy. "How could I forget!"

"Jesus..." I put my head in my hands. Appealing to Jax's better side is pointless. He doesn't have one. I've got to focus on what I need...and right now, that's my own goddamn house.

"Poker, huh? Maybe I can play in your stead..." I say. "Can we get someone to play in your stead?"

But Jax is shaking his head. "Supes only. And only the person who buys in can play."

"When is this game?" I ask.

"This weekend," he says.

"THIS WEEKEND?" I shout and the guards move closer. The one built like a house flexes his pecs at me in warning. I lower my voice. "*This weekend*, as in four days from now?"

He nods. "So...you should probably get started on getting me out of here," he says with a grin.

"I hate you so very much," I tell him. With a sigh, I add, "Okay, tell me about Kirkland, the guy who hired me. He obviously had a hand in setting you up. What do you know about him?"

"Yes. Good old Kirk. When I called him a friend, that probably wasn't the right word. More like a guy I met when I was out of work."

I try to keep from rolling my eyes. Jax has never held down what could be called a regular job. He's always working side hustles and dropping hints about the next big thing he has cooking. The one time it was meth, it was literally cooking, and he blew up a motor home in the process. The hilarious part, though, is that when I called him a drug dealer, he acted all offended. Told me, "Meth is important life-saving medicine." To this day I don't know if he believed that or just wanted me to.

"And what was this super awesome thing that your good friend Kirkland got you messed up in and landed you in jail?" I ask.

Jax leans forward, suddenly serious. "I was working for a group, sort of as a recruiter."

"Please do not tell me you're involved in trafficking," I say. I'd let him rot in here if that was the case.

"No, no, no," Jax waves his hands, dismissing my concerns. "It was all supes, consent required, of legal age."

"That's reassuring," I say drily. "Who were you working for?"

Jax hedges, looks around the room. The other jailbird and their visitors are talking quietly at their tables, not paying us any attention. His eyes light on a woman wearing an Ohio State University hoodie.

"O-H!" he yells at her, and she reflexively screams back, "I-O!"

Jax looks at me triumphantly, as if he's proven a point. "What?" I ask. "You went to jail and became a football fan? Are you trying to say you're recruiting supes to play college ball?"

"No!" Jax runs his hands over his face as if I'm being particularly dense, then yells at the woman again. "O-H!"

She yells back, "I-O!"

He gives me a hard stare, willing me to understand something.

"Ohio?" I hazard a guess and he instantly puts a finger to his lips.

"Don't say it!" he says, going white.

Confused, I ask, "Don't say...*Ohio*?"

His eyebrows fly up in alarm and he looks around the room again, exceedingly nervous. I am so done with his bullshit.

"What about Voldemort, can I say that?" I ask.

Jax makes a face. "Yeah, go ahead. Voldemort's not real, duh."

"But Ohio is, what, the state that cannot be named?"

Jax has his head in his hands now, and looks close to tears. It's kind of nice to be on the other end of a frustrating conversation with him, for once.

"Paige..." he whispers, leaning in closer to me. "I was working for the Order for Human Improvement Options."

"I've never heard of them," I say.

"Exactly," Jax says, leaning back as if he's proven his point.

"Sorry for being stupid," I say. "But you're going to have to spell this out for me. And I don't mean that literally," I have to add, as he goes to shout at the woman in the Buckeyes hoodie again.

"Fine," Jax says. "I met Kirkland, got to shooting the shit with him, and he tells me that I'd be a good recruiter for this group of humans that are looking for supes."

"What do they want supes for?"

Jax leans back in his chair and makes air quotes. "Opportunities."

I make them back. "Like what?"

Jax sighs. "I don't know. Like...stuff." He shrugs and then brightens. "They gave me a watch, a really nice one. And a brand-new TV. Not a cheapie either. When I watch porn it's like almost 3D, the picture is so clear."

I cross my arms. "Basically they gave you some free shit and you didn't ask any other questions except when you could start?"

He frowns at me. "Why do you say that like it's wrong?"

I sigh. "Because it sounds hella shady."

"You're just a suspicious person. How many times did you think I was cheating on you?"

"You *were* cheating on me!" I explode, slamming my hands onto the table.

Jax looks around at the people surrounding us with one of his impishly charming smiles. "Ex-wife," he explains. They nod, understanding. Focusing on me once more, he says in a lower voice, "Maybe it wasn't totally on the up and up. But what is these days? The money was real. And it was good. I was bringing supes in, getting a cut for each one, and was starting to really make some bank."

"Hold up," I say, bringing my hand up to get his attention because I can see he's on a roll. "You just told me that you were short on cash. That's why my house was collateral."

"You know how it is," Jax says, spreading out his hands. "Mo money, mo problems." He winks at me. "Pun intended."

My molars grind together. "That's not a pun. It's a saying."

"Isn't that what a pun is? Like you're always saying something and then adding 'pun intended.'"

"I only say that when what I've said is a pun. Like for example..." I take a moment to think. "Okay, you're gonna go to trial because they think you killed Kit. If the judge at your trial is a real talker, you better expect a long sentence."

Jax stares at me, totally serious. "What sort of sentence?"

I close my eyes and count to ten. If Jax and I were still married this is the point where I'd unzip his pants and remind myself of his finer features.

Finally I open my eyes again. Jax is making eyes at a busty woman across the room. I snap my fingers in front of his face. "Let's move on. You were recruiting supes and making good money. Then what happened?"

"Well, pretty soon I get to thinking, maybe I'm not getting enough. My hard work isn't really being appreciated."

"Now that I can believe," I say. Jax would feel like he's not getting his due even if he had a crown on his head and everyone had to bow to him before entering and exiting a room.

"I told Kirkland I wanted to meet up, talk about some advancement options for me. We got to drinking and talking, I told him how I felt and that I'd like to move a little higher up this ladder, and maybe there was a way to grease those wheels."

"Mixed metaphor," I call him out. "But keep going."

"He said it takes a lifetime to get to the inner circle, and that I'm not even in their orbit yet."

"I'm sure you took that well," I say. Jax likes to think that he's special. And that's a type of arrogance that was in his DNA long before he knew he was a supe.

Jax grimaces. "I kind of maybe said that if I didn't get what I wanted I'd talk to the media about them."

"Smart." I say, sarcastically. "How did Kirkland take that?"

"He said he'd pass my words up the chain and see what shook out. I told him the sooner the better because I could use some of that inner circle cash, being as I might soon lose my very-talented ex-wife's house right out from under her."

"And that's when he said he needed his house cleaned?" I ask.

"Yep. I told him where he could find you. I thought I was doing something good."

"Let me get this all straight," I say, "you threatened a member of a super secret organization with exposure unless you were recognized in a monetary way for your work, and then turned around and told him about your ex-wife. Who I am, what I do for a living, and where I could be found?"

Jax gives me a half-shrug. "Sorry. I think he spiked my drink with something. Like maybe a truth serum."

"Or maybe you're just that stupid." I rock back in my seat, thinking. "It still doesn't make sense why Kit was in that house. Shauna said he was into some shady stuff and she was following him, trying to keep his nose clean."

"Shauna!?" Jax asks. "She loved the shit out of Kit. And she already hates me enough as it is. If she thinks I killed him..."

"I'll handle it," I tell him. "Just like I always do."

"Thanks, Paige. I really should have treated you better," he tells me.

"You really should have," I say. I stand, and then pause. "If I do this, if I clear your name, I want the house...and I want you out of my life for good."

"Sure, anything..." he starts.

"I want a faerie bargain," I clarify.

His mouth clamps shut. Fae can't break a bargain. Not even Jax can wriggle his way out of one.

"Say it," I order. "Or you can rot in here forever. You know no one cares about another supe locked up. You know you won't get a fair trial. No. One. Cares," I repeat.

"I will make a bargain with you, Paige Harper. If you get me out of here in time for my game, I will put the deed to the house in your hands."

"And...?" I wait, arms crossed.

He swallows and I can see actual sorrow in his eyes. "And I will never darken your doorstep again."

"Deal," I say and reach out my hand.

Jax hesitates only slightly before taking it. "Deal," he says and a jolt of magic shoots up my arm.

My step is light as I leave the prison. I can get the house and Jax out of my life for good. All I have to do is find Kit's real killer. With zero leads.

I come crashing back down to earth. I need help.

And I know just the one-eyed werewolf who can give it to me.

11

Ms. Red Ferrari is just leaving Nico's office as I pull into the parking lot. She's got a definite sex bump in her hair and her lipstick is smeared. She doesn't even give me a sidelong glance until I slip past her and open Nico's door, then casually flip the OPEN sign to CLOSED. That oughta get her engine going. She might even put a P.I. on her P.I. so that she knows who he's fucking. I'm still smiling to myself when Nico comes out of the back, drying his hands on a paper towel.

"Keeping your clients happy?" I ask.

He laughs, then tosses the towel into the wastebasket. It sails cleanly in, of course. Apparently having only one working eye doesn't mess with his depth perception. Actually, I have a feeling he could make that shot with his eyes closed. Even if I didn't know Nico was a werewolf, I would know he was some sort of supe. There's an extra awareness about him. I can see it in the way he stands, shoulders low but not loose. And his chin is always slightly up, like he's smelling the air and knows exactly where everything is around him at all times.

It's intimidating. And also sorta hot. I can't help wondering if he's like Brent—always in control even when he's in bed. Or if that's the one place where he lets loose.

"I've got a business proposition for you," I say quickly, before I can follow that thought. About Nico. Or Brent. Especially Brent. I keep seeing him bending to pick up that ring. I wish I'd gotten a better look at it. Maybe even had it on my finger for just a second. Not that I'm itching to get married again. But I'm not immune to the magic of an engagement ring. Not literal magic, of course. Just the kind that little girls are socially conditioned to believe comes from a prince and happily ever afters. Jax should've cured me of caring about that stuff. He mostly did. And yet, I can't help wishing that Brent's proposal had gone the way he'd planned with the donuts and champagne and strawberries. I wish he'd gotten down on bended knee just so I could know what he would've said. And I wish—

"Have a seat," Nico says, interrupting my fantasy. He motions to the chair across from his desk. I sit, and realize the cushion is quite cold. Ms. Red Ferrari wasn't doing any sitting while she got the update on her case. "What can I help you with, Paige?"

I want to shoot back that I don't need his help, but that's an issue because I totally do. It's the whole reason why I'm here. I also want to tell him not to call me by my name, but that's stupid because it's my name. What is it about Nico Tralano makes me feel so contrary?! I end up buying time by gazing at the framed certificates behind his desk. Wait, is that one for massage therapy?

"What do you know about O.H.I.O?" I end up blurting out.

Nonplussed, Nico types something onto his computer, reads the results, then looks up at me and says, "It became a state in 1803. It's the 34th largest state in the union, and is in the Eastern time—"

"Cute." I cut him off. "But that's not what I mean."

Nico leans back in his chair, letting his eyes glide over me. It's an assessment, and while I've had plenty of men look at me in my life, I feel like Nico sees more with just one eye than they ever did with a pair.

"I honestly don't know what you mean, so why don't you just tell me why you're here, Paige Harper?"

I like it even less when he calls me by my full name. I cross my legs, and let my own gaze do some wandering. There are at least two shades of lipstick on Nico's collar, and unless he doesn't launder often (and judging by how good he smells, that's not a possibility), I gather he's had a very busy morning. Oddly enough, the skin around the collar starts to flush and I realize that Nico is blushing.

"O.H.I.O," I say, drawing myself back to the point at hand. "It's a secret organization, looking to recruit supes."

Nico's blush diminishes as soon as we start talking business, and he gives me a curt nod. "I've heard some rumors, but the name is new to me."

"Here's the deal," I say. "My ex-husband is not very bright."

Nico's lips twitch. "I do read the news," he says lightly.

"Yeah," I wince remembering that awful headline saying that I fingered my fae ex-husband. "Jax got himself involved with that group, O.H.I.O, as a recruiter. He was bringing in supes for...well, I don't know exactly what. To be honest, I don't think he knew either. But it seems he was doing pretty well for himself. And then, he got greedy."

Nico nods, pulls a yellow legal pad and a pen out of a drawer, and rolls his finger for me to keep going.

"He pushed for more inclusion, or access to the inner

circle, or more money or..." I know I'm rambling. I must look like an idiot. Nico hasn't even written down anything I've said, probably dismissing it all as babble and waiting for me to finally admit that really I just came in here because I'd love to know if the package behind that zipper delivers like the postal service—rain, sleet or snow.

"Your ex got in over his head?" Nico prompts me. "And now he's in jail for murder."

"Exactly," I say. "But he didn't do it. He was set up, by a guy named Kirkland."

The pen jumps in his hand, and I know I just said the right thing. I've got Nico's full attention now. "That's the fae I warned you about. The one who was in your office late the other night," he says.

I nod. "You said he works for Oberon. But that information was either wrong or outdated."

"Outdated...maybe," Nico says, and I can tell he doesn't want to admit that there is something he was wrong about. "But I know for sure, no matter who he works for, that is not a fae to tangle with."

"He is not someone with whom one should tangle," I say.

Nico frowns. "That's what I just said."

"No," I give a slight shake of my head. "You said something similar but your sentence arrangement ended on a preposition. Which isn't incorrect, but should be avoided when one is able."

Nico gives me a hard stare and grumbles something under his breath that sounds a bit like, "Fucking English majors."

Honestly, I don't care about where prepositions land in a sentence. I do, however, like getting under Nico's skin. I want him to know I'm not like the other ladies who come in here ready to drop their panties at a wink of his eye. Sure, I can see he's attractive. And yes, hearing him "working" next door it's difficult to keep myself from being curious about his client's satisfaction—especially when he clearly has repeat customers. But what a girl wonders about and what she does are two totally different things. And my nether regions are never ever ever gonna meet with Nico's.

"So, Jax pissed off Kirkland," Nico says, pulling me back to the topic at hand. "And you want me to look into it?"

"Yes! I don't even know where to start." I admit.

Nico's one eye is boring into me. "Are you sure he was framed?"

"I wasn't at first. But now, yes. The whole thing makes zero sense." I tell him what I know. "It's too convenient. Even how the vamp was taking blood thinners. And I know all about the serial killer." I say, when Nico looks like he's about to interrupt. He seems surprised, but then nods, giving me another once over. But this one feels like it's drilling down into my brain, intrigued to have found something of worth there.

"Jax can barely juggle one scam at a time, much less be organized enough to commit multiple homicides," I say.

"Your ex is definitely not the serial killer," Nico says, like he's imparting wisdom.

"No shit, Arthur Conan Doyle," I shoot back, and he actually grins. Oh my God, did he just get my literary joke?

"I've actually been hired to find out who *is*," Nico goes on, and it's my turn to be surprised. "It seems, my dear Watson, your case and mine might just be linked."

"There's some proper grammar!" I say, unable to resist the urge to poke at him again.

His eyes narrow slightly and his grin grows feral.

"Imagine that, from a common slob like me who technically never even graduated from high school."

My eyebrows go up as I realize that I've touched a sore spot. "You could always get your GED," I offer sweetly.

"You know what?. I'm doing just fine without it. In fact, business has been real good lately."

He draws out the word real, almost taunting me with it. Daring me even. I know that if I correct him again, he's not gonna just let it pass.

"Really," I say softly. "Business has been really good."

Nico stands abruptly, his chair screeching. And then he's on the other side of the desk, looming over me. I don't flinch, but I do lean back into my chair, trying to put as much space as possible between us. That's impossible, though, as Nico sits on the edge of the desk directly in front of me. He manspreads so that his crotch is in front of my face. Reminding myself that I need his help, I don't attempt to put my fist into his balls. His knee brushes against my crossed legs as he leans forward, further into my space.

"If we're gonna work together, Paige, then we gotta be on the same page." His voice is low. Intimate. Or maybe he's just speaking softly because we're so close that any other volume would be like him shouting in my face. "Pun intended," he adds in a way that would make my knees weak if it was any other man.

Okay fine, even with this werewolf of a man, it still makes my knees weak.

I want to scoot my chair back. Or stand and walk away. But that would be equal to surrender. Because we're locked in a contest right now and the first one to blink loses.

"I'm so glad you think so," I agree with faux sweetness. Leaning forward, I place my hand on his thigh. His upper thigh. It tightens beneath my fingertips. The pads of my fingers slide across denim and then the tips of my fingers curl so that my pink-painted fingernails are the only part touching him.

"Just so we're clear. I'm not helping Jax out of the kindness of my heart. "It's not kind. *I'm* not kind." I apply pressure, letting my fingernails press into Nico's leg. He swallows. Hard. His Adam's apple bobbing. But he doesn't move away. And I don't either. "The reason why I'm here is very self-serving," I continue.

"Is it?" Nico asks, and I can see him wondering if this is the part where I tell him that I need a good fuck to clear my head. Or whatever it is his clients say to let him know a little werewolf strange is what they need to heal their broken hearts.

But I'm not like those desperate chumps. I'm Paige Harper. A survivor. And I bend to no one. Especially not a supe, I don't care that there's a rising bulge in his jeans and I don't just mean a bump. There are some situations where having a good vocabulary is a benefit, and that thing is a protuberance.

My fingernails press harder into Nico's thigh. "I am not letting any fae, man, or werewolf get the best of me ever again," I tell him as I rake my fingernails up his leg and end right before they'd travel to a markedly higher elevation. "Any man who tries will see his balls hang from my rearview mirror."

Nico's eyes widen and then, amazingly, he laughs. He pushes at my shoulder and despite the lightness of the tap, I easily stumble back into my chair. He moves away, giving me space once more.

"Paige Harper, not a woman to mess with," he says softly. He sounds impressed, but also...he emphasizes that last word. With. Letting me know that I might've won this round, but I shouldn't get too comfortable.

I take a small moment to savor my win and then get back to business.

"Another thing. Jax staked the house where I live for a buy-in at an underground supe poker game. He can't transfer his seat, and the game is in four days."

"The Titan Hold-Em?" Nico asks, his brow furrowing. "That's a serious group of fiends. They'll take your house, and you, if you're still in it when they get there."

"They aren't getting it," I say, grinding my teeth. "That is *my* house, and nobody else has a right to it. Except Jax, because he currently holds the deed. And possibly the man I have as a housemate. And also a coked-up pixie ex-sister-in-law. If she comes back. But that's it," I insist, pointing at Nico to deliver on intensity.

His mouth quivers as if he's about to laugh, but thinks better of it. "Like I said, I've got a stake in this, too. I've got some good sources among the police, but if the top brass want to pin the vamp killings on Jax, my tips will dry up. I trust my intel, but they'll fall into line if they're told to. Not everyone has the moxie to go up against power."

Now I feel like I might be the one to blush.

"I'll go up against anyone," I say, then realize that was horrible wording as Nico smirks. "I mean, I won't go down on anyone." I sigh and try again. "I won't back down from a fight," I clarify.

Nico nods, his face serious again. "I'm starting to get that." There's almost admiration in his voice and it makes me more uncomfortable than the smirk.

I jump up from my chair, ready to leave. Nico follows me to the door, flipping the sign back to OPEN without a comment.

"I want to be a part of the investigation," I tell him. "I want to work *with* you. I'm a little strapped for cash right now, but I can pay...what is your fee?"

"Don't worry about that right now. I'll give you the friends' discount." His smile is disarming.

"We are not friends," I tell him. "And don't try to be charming," I add. "It's not one of your strengths."

His eyebrows go up and I realize that I might've gone a little too far. From friendly sparring into actually being mean. But we're not friends. I meant that. So why do I even care?

Nico holds the door open for me and as I pass by him I get a whiff of his scent. In a better world he'd stink like the little toy poodle I grew up with who was prone to anal gland infections. But Nico has more of a musky man smell. In a good way. In too good of a way. Resisting the urge to take a deeper breath, I hurry past.

"We should compare notes," Nico says before I can disappear into my own office. "What are you doing tonight?"

"I'm available," I say, then quickly amend that statement. "I'm free, I mean. I've got nothing going on tonight."

"Good, me neither," Nico says, reaching past me to open the door. "And Paige... you don't need to clarify yourself. I know you're not available."

I pause halfway through the door, a ripple of electricity running up my spine as I feel his breath on my neck.

"I can smell him on you." There's a little bit of a growl in his voice, like maybe he doesn't like it. The sound vibrates down my spine like it just tapped into the motherlode. I don't want to keep walking and pretend like I didn't hear him, but I don't want to turn around either. I'm not ready to go toe to toe with him again. Or fingernails to crotch. Luckily, a little black Trans Am jets into the parking lot, pulling to a stop in front of his office. A pretty young thing gets out, her gaze gliding over us, a spark of jealousy immediately catching.

"Looks like your next client is here to be serviced," I say lightly, ignoring the little bolt of irritation that ignites in my own gut.

"What time should I pick you up tonight?" Nico asks calmly.

"It isn't a date," I protest, finally turning around.

"Of course not," he says. "But a man's gotta eat."

My mouth works as I try to come up with a response, and Nico leans in closer to whisper in my ear.

"And a werewolf has to eat even more."

12

———

After talking to Nico, I bill the police department for the cleanup, then go home. I doubt any calls I get today will be about work. I already have three messages from journalists asking to interview *me* about fingering my ex-husband. They all use that exact word —*fingering*.

When I get home, Darron and Shauna are sitting at the dining room table drinking coffee and eating cookies.

"You're back," I say warily.

"I didn't have anywhere else to go," she tells me, looking down into her cup. "All my friends say that I've burned too many bridges and until I get cleaned up they can't help me." She takes a sip, grimaces, then pours in at least a cup of sugar. "Which is totally unfair. I didn't even burn that bridge. I exploded it into eensy weensy tiny pieces."

I take a deep breath and sit with them. Of course it's up to me. I'm going to have to tell her about Kit all over again. But before I can gather the courage, Darron speaks up.

"We were just talking about our wives. I think they would have been friends," he says, with a wink at Shauna.

I nod. Shauna's wife disappeared in the Ghosting. But Darron...I realize he's mentioned his wife before but I never asked what happened to her.

"Wife?" I ask, then my brain registers that he said, 'would have been.' As in, past tense.

He looks into his cup and says sadly, "I lost her in the Ghosting. We were actually out with a few friends at brunch. One minute we're sucking down mimosas and French toast and the next, poof. She's gone. I miss her so incredibly much."

I nod. "My parents ghosted too."

"I know, dear," Darron tells me. "It's just unbelievably tragic." He shakes his head, but then gives me a sad smile. "Do you want some coffee? It's fresh."

"Better not," I tell him. I'm already wired. I study Shauna who is looking into her cup. "Shauna. I have some...bad news."

"About Kit?" she asks sadly.

I nod. "Do you remember?"

"I didn't at first, but, I think...Paige, is Kit dead?" She starts to cry.

"He is. I'm so sorry." Darron gets up and rubs Shauna's back. She's so small, she looks like a child.

"You can stay here until you get on your feet," I tell her before I can stop myself.

All this after I made such a show to Nico of insisting that I'm not a nice person. I remind myself that he doesn't need to know that my pixie ex-sister-in-law is staying with me.

"Thanks, Paige," Shauna sniffles. "I got a call from the police. I must have been listed as Kit's emergency contact. I didn't listen to the message. I just...I can't."

"Do you want me to listen first?" Darron offers.

She hands him the phone gratefully. "I just...I'm not

good at dealing with stuff since Tina vanished. I've been hitting the beauty pretty hard."

Darron nods. "I drank myself asleep quite a few times after the ghosting. Just be careful. You don't want to take so much beauty that you never wake up. It's rare, but it's possible that instead of sleeping off a beauty binge, the fae can go into a coma."

"What does it matter?" Shauna asks. "Everyone I love is gone."

"I felt that way too," I admit. "My parents were always there for me. Then they were just...not. But you have to live for yourself," I tell her.

She gives me a pitying smile. "Parents are supposed to kick the bucket. But Tina was my wife. And a vampire. She should have lived forever!" Shauna ends on a pathetic wail. I have to resist the urge to slap her upside the head. At least physically. But there's no holding me back from reminding her, "My parents did not kick the bucket. They disappeared."

I spit the words at her, but Shauna just shrugs in response. She's only half paying attention to me as she watches Darron. Shauna's phone is pressed to his ear and his expression is grave as he listens to the message.

"Let's not play 'whose pain is worse,'" Darron gently suggests as he finally sets the phone down. Reaching across the table, he takes Shauna's hands in his. "You're the only lead they have on his identity. He didn't have any I.D. on him. They want you to come down to the station and identify him."

Shauna shakes her head. "I can't. I can't see him like that."

"I'll come with you," I volunteer, hoping I might get some clues that will help me clear Jax, like maybe a note in

Kit's pocket with the name and address of the person who killed him. That would be helpful. "I have to tell you, I really don't think Jax did this."

"I don't think so either," Shauna says. "But whoever did is going to have to answer to me." She squeezes her coffee cup and it shatters; sugary globs spill down her arm and onto the table.

Darron jumps up to grab a dish cloth while Shauna sucks on her fingers. The small cuts almost immediately disappear and I remind myself that Shauna is a vampire-fae hybrid. A double supe.

She's going to be double the trouble.

I pull Darron aside and tell him about the house being used as collateral in a poker game. I don't want him to live here, but he deserves to know that his situation is precarious at best.

He shakes his head. "That scheming bastard..."

I nod. If anyone can empathize with being frustrated with Jax, it's me.

"Maybe I can play..." he starts. But I shake my head.

"I already thought of that. But it's supes only."

"So what are we going to do?" he asks. I have to say, with his use of we, Darron is growing on me.

"I'm going to get Jax out of jail and to that game," I tell him.

"I don't think Jax killed anyone, but getting him out by the weekend is going to be a tall order," he tells me.

"I know. I hired a P.I. And let's see if I can learn anything from going with Shauna to identify the body."

"Good luck," Darron tells me as I usher Shauna out the door. "You are sure going to need it."

When we arrive at the coroner's, Shauna is immediately a wreck. She starts shivering and crosses her arms over her chest as we head down the green-tiled hallway. I put my arm around her shoulders but she's shaking so hard her wings are vibrating.

The guard at the check-in desk gives us a glance, taking in her wings. "You here for the dead supe?"

I feel a brief flash of rage on Shauna's behalf; it wouldn't hurt the guy to have a little compassion. But I needn't bother; Shauna's already on him, hot and heavy. She snaps into her tiny pixie form, her small hand shaking under his nose.

"You here to get fisted in the nostril?" she threatens.

"That's a new one," a voice behind us says, and I turn to see Detective McGinnis coming toward us. "It's good to see you again."

"Good to see you, too," I say, actually meaning it. McGinnis is the guy with an English major wife, and I didn't catch him checking me out even once. Granted, I had blood all over me, but most guys that are going to sneak a peek don't have high standards.

McGinnis tilts his head. "It's not often the wife of the assailant shows up with the deceased's family to identify the victim."

"It's complicated," I tell him. Shit, I'm going to have to amend my statement. Except everything I told him was true, I just no longer think it's the entire truth. "I want to talk to you about what I witnessed..."

McGinnis takes a step forward, "Are you being pressured by anyone to lie?"

"No. No nothing like that." Shauna zooms forward and

snaps back into her larger form. "It's just also very complicated."

McGinnis turns to Shauna. "You must be the relative of the deceased?"

"Yes," she says, staring at him suspiciously when he holds out a hand for her to shake. She takes it reluctantly, her smaller hand dwarfed in his massive one, and pulls back slowly, as if she's surprised he didn't give her an electric shock or something. Huh...maybe supes are just as frightened of humans as we are of them. Given some of what I've seen of the Firsters, I can't say I blame them.

Then I remember Nico's hot breath on my neck, the low growl in his throat. The fear that ran up my spine. No, supes definitely have the upper hand, and I can't ever forget that.

"I'm sorry for your loss," McGinnis says, then nods at the desk guard. "I'll take these ladies in."

We follow him into a room that looks like it's lined with filing cabinets...except I know from late night crime show binges that they aren't for paperwork. McGinnis pulls one open and a sheeted body slides out, along with a cold puff of air. He goes to the head, but pauses before pulling back the sheet.

"I'll need a positive identification from you," he tells Shauna, "After that I can give you some time alone with him."

Shauna nods that she understands, then starts shaking again. I put my arm around her, and hold her against me, trying to give her warmth and support. McGinnis pulls back the cover, and I notice that he doesn't take it below the neck, sparing Shauna the sight of the killing wound.

She gasps, folds into me a little, her wings beating like a stuttering heart. "Yes," she says, wiping her eyes. "That's him. That's my brother Kit."

"I'm sorry for your loss," McGinnis says, reaching across the body to give Shauna's wrist a squeeze. Amazingly, she lets him.

He turns to me. "I'll leave you to it. Take as much time as you need."

I nod, and Shauna reaches for Kit's face, adjusting a lock of his hair. "I'm so sorry," she whispers. "I'm sorry I didn't do more for you. I'm sorry I didn't realize what kind of trouble you were in. And I'm sorry I didn't try harder to help you get out."

"Get out?" I repeat. "Shauna, what do you mean? What was Kit into?"

She shakes her head, tiny, pearlescent tears forming on her lashes. "He got involved with some sort of...I don't know what it was. Some kind of money-making scheme, too good to be true. I wanted in, but he said no. That got all my alarms going off. I told him if it was too shady to bring me in, I didn't want *him* to have anything to do with it. I should have known how bad it was, because he let slip that humans were involved. I mean, you really just can't trust humans." She pauses a beat and seems to remember that I am human. Flashing a smile that shows her tiny sharp teeth, she adds, "No offense."

My own bells are going off like a five-alarm fire. "This organization, was it called O.H.I.O, by any chance?"

"I don't know." She shakes her head. "He said it was super-secret and he couldn't really tell me much. Kit and I didn't keep secrets from each other. I thought he was abandoning me like everyone else. That he thought I was too much of a mess to be trusted. But now...." She sniffs miserably. "Now I think he was just trying to keep me safe."

"I'm so sorry," I say, wishing there were better words.

Shauna's pain is so sharp and fresh, it's almost visible

around her. Before I lost my parents I wouldn't have recognized it. That inner throbbing pain that makes a person stand and talk and even breathe differently. But now having gone through it—and still dealing with it—it's easier to recognize in others.

I also know the only thing I can do to help her is just stand here and listen.

"We had a big fight the last time I saw him," Shauna whispers like it's a confession. "I told him he was falling for the oldest game in town, and a human one, too. I said I didn't want anything to do with it, even though that was a lie. I was just so mad he wouldn't let me in." She scrunches her face up, thinking. "I might have even called him a human whore."

"Sorry about that," she says to her brother's body.

"And what did he say?" I prod, feeling terrible for taking advantage of her talkative mood, but also needing answers.

"He said that I didn't need to take care of him anymore. That I couldn't even if I wanted to, because I could barely take care of myself." Her voice changes and I can hear her getting angry again as she remembers Kit's words. "He said it was time for *him* to take care of *me*." Shauna glares down at Kit. Sticking a finger out, she pokes his chest. "And look where that got you. This is why I watched out for you. You may be a big bad vamp, but you're still my little brother." Shauna breaks down in sobs, flinging her body on top of Kit's.

I take a step back and let her have a moment alone with her brother. When her tears subside, I gently peel her off him.

"You did watch out for him," I remind her softly. "You put that app on his phone, the tracking one."

Shauna gives a shaky laugh. "He would've been so

pissed if he found out about that. Luckily, Kit was terrible with tech. We weren't raised with it in Faerieland. My wife Tina taught me a lot, though—" Shauna gasps, as if the added weight of these two losses has stolen her breath.

"The app is why you showed up at the house," I say, prodding her onward and hoping I don't push her into a total emotional collapse with my questions. "Can you remember anything else he might have said?"

"No, not specifically. But I know he got cold feet. He left me a voicemail one night, clearly spooked. He said if I ever got a phone call saying he was in trouble or hurt, not to believe it, that someone was just trying to lure me out."

My heart thuds hard at this. Jax said he was at the house because of someone calling to say I was hurt. It's not exactly proof, but it's the best indicator yet that they were both involved with the same shady folks.

"I can't see him like this anymore," Shauna says abruptly, flipping the sheet over Kit's face. I close the cupboard, rolling Kit back into his chilly storage drawer.

"C'mon," I say, wrapping my hands around her arm and steering her toward the door. "Let's get out of here."

"I hadn't heard from him for a few days," Shauna says as we walk, and I can tell she's replaying the days before she found Kit. And thinking of all the things she could've done differently. All the ways she might have saved him. "I should've known something was wrong, but we'd had that fight and I was sucking down so much beauty, I kinda lost track of time. But then I got a notification from the tracker app. He was at a location way outside his usual spots. So I followed him, and that's when I ran into you."

A bubble of hope rises in me as I realize the tracker must've been a pretty decent one if it was making note of the places he normally went. It could be the key to figuring this whole thing out. I might not even need Nico. "Which app were you using?" I ask. "And for how long did you have it on his phone? If we could backtrack his movements..."

"I just put it on his phone a week ago." She reaches into her back pocket, pulling out her phone. "Philanderer Follower," she says, turning her phone around to show me the app, which features a stick figure with a boner and two x's for eyes. "It lists everywhere he's been. That way if you don't catch him in the act, you can at least catch him in a lie — Oh!" Her face lights up as she suddenly realizes. "I can use this to find his killer, can't I?"

"Maybe..." I hedge, as vengeance fills Shauna's little face. Silently I curse myself for not being more careful with information. I thought she was lost in her grief and I could just ease the phone out of her hands and use it to clear Jax's name. Obviously, I didn't realize how mercurial her moods can be, because Shauna has gone from a pathetic tragic mess to a creature of fight and fury.

Her eyes glow with a manic glee. "When I find the fucker I'm going to explode him like a fart in a smoke monster!"

Shit. How do I rein in an off-the-rails pixie? "Look, Shauna...I think you should let me handle this." Her head snaps up, the crazy in her wide eyes scaring me. "Because," I hurriedly continue, "Darron was super low after he opened up about his wife. You guys hit it off. I need you to go make sure that he's okay."

I attempt to take the phone from her but she holds on tight. For someone so small, she's got a hell of a grip. Leaning into it, I tug again. This time, though, Shauna lets go. I stumble back a few steps and only barely manage to keep from falling on my ass.

Still, the phone is in my hand. At least for the moment.

But Shauna is advancing on me with narrowed eyes. "Are you trying to get rid of me?"

"No! Of course not," I lie. "You obviously need to make the person who did this to Kit pay."

Shauna nods. "So why are you stopping me?"

"I'm not! I'm just, uh..." My brain spins wildly, looking for something that will appease her. "I don't want you to waste it. I mean sure, it would feel good to explode the person like a, uh, fart in a—"

"Smoke monster," Shauna says. "It's a real thing."

"I don't doubt it. The thing is, you can only kill this person once. And that seems like a horrible yet quick way to go. Maybe you want to make this person suffer a little longer?"

I can't believe the words coming out of my mouth. I'm supposed to be cleaning up this crap, not helping someone plan it.

But Shauna very much likes what I've got to say. "You're right," she says. Lost in thought, she stares up at the ceiling and muses aloud. "I could get a witch involved. I'll hurt. The witch will heal. Then I can hurt some more."

I clear my throat, interrupting her thoughts. "Clearly, you have some planning to do. In the meantime, why not let me do the legwork, then I'll call you in after we figure out who...who killed your brother."

She narrows her eyes at me and I think I'm about ready to have the grandmother of arguments, but then her face softens. "Yeah, okay." She plucks back her phone. "I'll download the app on your phone, though, log you in as me." She holds out her hand.

I'm so grateful, I give her my phone with a sigh of relief.

I see McGinnis lurking near the end of the hallway so I take Shauna's elbow and steer her his way while she fiddles with my phone. "You wanted to change your statement?" McGinnis asks me.

"No. Yes. I don't know," I say. "Look, I know that Jax didn't kill anyone. He was framed."

"I agree," McGinnis tells me. It takes me a moment to process what he said.

"You do?" I ask. "Then why is Jax even in custody?!" Maybe there's hope for me getting him out in time to save the house after all.

"Because someone high up is very interested in keeping him locked up," he whispers. My hope deflates.

McGinnis looks up and down the hall, then pulls me to the side. "I don't know what you and your ex got wrapped up in, but they are trying to turn him into the vampire Ted Bundy. Not just that poor boy's murder, but all the vamps that have showed up dead recently."

"You know this is wrong," I tell him.

He gives me a curt nod. "I'm a good cop. I know a lot of good cops, but..." Again he looks around. "This is fishy as a Friday night fish fry."

"What can we do?" I ask.

"*We* can't do anything. I'm the lead detective on the case and I've been told that your fae hubs Jax is our man. I have a wife and kids and I'm not going to rock the boat, not when it means the ones I love could drown." I close my eyes. I understand why McGinnis wouldn't want to put his family in danger. Not for a dead vamp and a framed fae.

"But," he continues, "if someone outside of the law were to get undeniable proof and make that public, there's nothing that we could do to cover it up, really. Not if, say, the media got wind of it." He stares at me pointedly.

I nod. McGinnis can't help. This is on me.

"I'm rooting for you," he tells me. "I wish there was more I could do."

"I appreciate it," I tell him. And I do. Even if he's not helping, just sharing information might be enough to endanger him.

I already suspected it, but now it's becoming more and more clear. This thing I'm going after is big, and if I'm not careful it'll take me down too.

13

I stand in front of my closet, considering my options. I'm not trying to impress Nico, I'm suiting up for battle. And that means wearing something that is going to make me feel good. Like the kind of woman who can go toe to toe with a werewolf and come out on top.

An involuntary vision of me riding Nico pops into my head.

I quickly banish it and remind myself that such thoughts are not self-fulfilling. If they were, I would've married Chris Hemsworth instead of Jax.

Sighing, I pull out a pair of reliable jeans that make my ass look really good, but also could be passed off as me just having a nice ass. A little black tee with a scoop neck hints at cleavage without spilling it over the top. I stick with my usual ponytail but dress it up a bit, tying it back with a red ribbon.

I look very much like my cartoon Down & Dirty logo. Every now and then I am recognized on the street, thanks to a pouty TV ad we shot when I was about ten years younger.

It still can be found on YouTube, and I get calls about it sometimes. Some of them are even for cleaning gigs.

Point is, I look good. And I know it. I head to the restaurant feeling confident. I have a very attractive ex-husband, and very nearly had an equally attractive almost-husband. There is no reason Nico Tralano should be able to fluster me.

I get to the restaurant first, and take a table facing the door, so that I can spot him as soon as he walks in. Nico and I agreed to a Mexican restaurant that's known for its margaritas. They've knocked me on my ass more than once. When the waiter asks me if I'd like a drink, I hesitate a moment and then order iced tea. Best to keep my wits about me, with a werewolf sitting across from me.

Turns out I don't need to see the door to know when Nico arrives. Heads turn. Mostly lady heads, but a few dudes, too.

I give him a once-over and realize either he spent a lot of time trying to look casual and ended up looking hot as shit too, or he just always looks this way. Somehow he makes an eyepatch the must-have accessory of the season. He spots me and makes his way to the table, earning me a few envious glares.

"Paige," he says, giving me a nod. "Would you mind switching seats with me? I like to have my eye on the door."

My immediate impulse is to just be nice and do it. Of course, because it's Nico asking, I decide not to. He sure does make my contrary side show up.

"Doesn't it make more sense for me to watch the door? I mean, I have two eyes," I point out faux sweetly.

"Fair point," he says, and sits down. "But let's agree on a signal if any members of Lucifer's Ladies show up. I'll need a microsecond lead."

"Lucifer's Ladies?" I ask, glancing up from the menu.

"It's a female motorcycle gang with a price on my head," he says, as he casually surveys the wine list.

"Ooooh," I say. "What are you worth? And is it dead or alive? I could use a paint job on the van."

"Definitely alive," he answers. "In this case, *price on my head* has a different meaning."

My eyebrows rise several inches. "Clarify."

Nico sighs. "I did a job for them a while back—"

"Oh god, you slept with them," I say.

"Actually, I didn't." Nico frowns at me. "I don't sleep with all my clients, you know."

"That's not what I hear." I cup a hand around one of my ears. "And I literally hear quite a bit. I assumed you had some sort 'get your clients off' guarantee."

Half of Nico's mouth curls upward as he leans in across the table. "Do you like to listen, Paige?"

"No!" My voice is oddly high and strained. I sound like I did as a huffy teenager denying to my mom that I'd been looking at the illustrated Kama Sutra cards my parents kept in a bedside drawer.

My mom wasn't convinced and I don't think Nico is either because the other side of his mouth edges up to join the first. "There's no official guarantee, but apparently Lucifer's Ladies heard the same thing you did and now think they missed out. They say I owe them a night."

I frown at this. It was fun teasing Nico, but this... "Sounds kinda rapey," I say aloud.

Nico shrugs it off. "Nah. It's fine. Anyway, you know how it is for pretty people like us. Everyone wants a piece."

I'd been in the middle of taking a sip of my iced tea, but with Nico's words it goes down the wrong tube and I choke. I never considered myself in the same category of pretty as

Nico. That he seems to think otherwise is both disturbing...and flattering.

And then I ruin the whole thing by coughing so hard that it feels like I might dislodge one of my lungs. Of course, Nico comes around to my side of the table to pound on my back. Recovering, I wave him back to his seat, but by that time I'm red-faced and my nose is running.

Well at least he only said I was "pretty" and didn't add "suave" or "cool under pressure."

The waiter saves me, arriving with a giant basket of chips, salsa, and one of those ridiculously gigantic margaritas with two straws sticking out the top of it.

"Your usual," the waiter tells Nico with a wink.

I peer around the gigantic drink to give him my most dry look. "You bring women here a lot?"

He doesn't even have the decency to look embarrassed as he reaches for a chip and digs into the salsa. "I can't resist the bottomless basket of chips."

"Well, I'm not drinking tonight," I tell him, and then realizing I sound like a total prude and a stick in the mud too, I try to clarify. "This is business. We don't want to get confused."

There's a hint of the predator in the return smile Nico gives me. "Are you in danger of getting confused, Paige? Because I swear, no matter how sloppy drunk you get, it wouldn't even occur to me to take advantage of you."

"Oh it wouldn't, would it?" I retort.

So much for Nico considering me 'one of the pretty people.' I always assumed he'd never tried to make a move on me because I was giving off 'I will gouge out your eyeballs with my fingernails' vibes, but maybe he's just never been interested. The idea is actually a little funny. I've spent all this time worrying I might accidentally end up in Nico's bed, when he doesn't even want me there.

The hell with it then.

I tug at one of the straws and bring my lips to it, sucking down the tart drink. The tequila hits me first and then the tang of lime. But with the straw, I didn't get any salt. I swipe some from the rim with the tip of my finger and stick it in my mouth, sucking the salt off.

A whisper-soft growl reminds me that Nico is on the other side of the table. He's watching me. No, he's watching my finger. And my lips pursed around it. For a moment I freeze as our eyes meet. Then I pull my finger loose with a light pop.

Nico swallows.

Or maybe he wouldn't kick me out of his bed. I've never gotten such mixed signals from a guy in my life. Not that it matters, I once again remind myself.

Desperate to get that dark hungry look out of Nico's eyes, I change the subject. "So Lucifer's Ladies are what...harpies? Is that why you're not interested in sleeping with them?"

Nico blinks and then seems to refocus. "Harpies? No, they're just normal ladies. Humans. If they were harpies..." Nico shakes his head and a distant look comes over his face, like he's remembering something.

"What?" I say, curious despite myself.

"Harpies are notoriously independent," he says.

"And ugly," I add. "Like withered old lady birds."

Nico shrugs. "Sure, using only your eyes, they're ugly. But when they're interested in someone they emit these pheromones that..." Nico sniffs deeply, as if he can smell it. "Most harpies are asexual. They don't need men to procreate, so most don't even have a sex drive. But the rare ones that do are known for being the best lovers on the planet."

I squint at Nico, fairly sure that he's bullshitting me. Then again...I've heard stranger things.

"So the group that's chasing you is just normal ladies," I say.

"Not normal ladies," Nico says with a shudder. "I think they were all happy housewives before the ghosting. But now..."

"Now they're horny hell on wheels?" I guess.

Nico laughs. "I guess you could say that."

"Well, don't worry about those Lucifer's Ladies," I tell him. "You're safe with me."

"Am I?" he asks, spreading both arms along the back of the booth. It shows off his shoulders, and stretches the tee across his chest. And rib cage. I think I can see the outline of his belly button. Wait...do werewolves have belly buttons? I have a sudden desire to find out.

"Are you ready to order?" the waiter asks.

"Yes," I say a little too emphatically. I actually have no idea what I want so I just point at the only salad on the menu. Nico gets twenty steak tacos. When he notices me staring, he tells me, "They're small," and then turns to the waiter and amends his order to twenty-five. Clearly, Nico was not kidding about werewolves needing to eat more.

"Business must be good," I observe, as the waiter leaves. "You can afford meat."

"I'm in a line of business that does well when people tell lies," Nico says.

"Total job security," I say.

"And you're in a line of business that does well when they create messes," he goes on. "Also lucrative, I assume."

"I do okay." I shrug. I don't add more. I don't need Nico Tralano up in my business any more than he is already.

"You should know that I went to school with Shauna's wife," he tells me. "Ages ago. She...well, we had our problems. I actually hated vampires. I wasn't a good guy back then."

"You were a lone wolf?" I ask, and he groans.

"Something like that. My head was pretty messed up with what it meant to be a werewolf. I realized I didn't want to be like that anymore."

"I don't think less of you for hating vampires," I tell him. I don't add that all supes are high on my list of things I despise. "But...wait...you're not the vamp serial killer, are you?" I ask, making sure my voice shows that I'm joking. "That would be messed up, if you're investigating the murders that you committed."

He shakes his head, flashing a toothy smile. "No, I made my peace with vampires a long time ago. Buried the hatchet with Tina as well. At the time of the ghosting, there was no longer any bad blood between us.

"Well then, you know Shauna?" I ask.

"I've met her briefly. She's a pistol."

"Tell me about it!"

"I will, one day. I have a few fae stories up my sleeve," he says, getting a little too chummy for my liking.

"Shauna and I went to the morgue this afternoon," I tell Nico, getting down to business. "She identified Kit, and told me that he was also involved with a group that sounds a lot like O.H.I.O, though she didn't know their name. She was worried he'd gotten in over his head with something, so she put a tracking app on his phone."

"Which one?" Nico asks, eyebrows drawn.

"Philanderer Follower," I tell him, and he groans.

"That thing is going to put me out of business."

"I wouldn't worry," I tell him. "I don't think many of your clients are really all that worried about where their husbands are. They just like doing "business" with you."

"That's exactly what I mean," he says. "Philandering goes both ways, Paige."

I almost choke a little bit on my tea, but am spared answering when the waiter arrives with our food. We eat in silence for a few minutes.

"Wow, you're really *wolfing* down your food," I say, and he glances up, a dab of green salsa on his lip that I feel the urge to take my napkin and wipe off.

"Funny," he says. "You're really *nursing* that tea."

I shake my head, take a sip. "Doesn't work. I'm not a nurse."

"It's a stretch," he admits. "But I can't really say you're *humaning* anything."

I sigh dramatically, lean back in my seat. "Nico, if we're going to work together, you're going to have to get better at puns."

"You want us to work together more?" he says.

I roll my eyes and pick at my food. Nico calls over the waiter, whispers something to him, then sends him on his way. I don't have time to ask what that was about before Nico starts talking.

"This app. You're thinking we can backtrack the victim's movements?"

"Shauna says so, yes. I already ran the last few addresses Kit was at; one is a Whole Foods, one is a condemned industrial building on the wharf. Two guesses which one I think is more promising."

"You'd be surprised what goes on at Whole Foods," Nico says with a straight face.

"I was once hired to clean up after a manticore mating meetup," I tell him. "Nothing surprises me. The last place Kit visited was a residential address. Shauna says it's not Kit's house. But he *did* spend the night there."

"Philanderer Follower comes through," Nico observes wryly. "Did he have a girlfriend, or a boyfriend?"

"Not that he ever mentioned to Shauna," I say as the waiter returns carrying a gigantic burrito. He places it in front of me.

"I didn't order this," I say, but Nico stops me.

"My treat." He grins and I want to be contrary and say I'm not going to eat his meat or something clever, but it smells so freaking good. I scoop it up and take a gigantic bite. The thing is filled with giant chunks of seared steak, perfectly cooked. I moan with pleasure.

I expect Nico to make a rude comment but he just devours his own tacos. After I demolish mine I lick my fingers and sit back happily. I realize that this is meant to be a business dinner and I feel bad for getting lost in the moment. I sit up.

Nico wipes his hands on his napkin, tossing it onto the table, and smiles. "Paige Harper," he muses. "You're the first human in a long time to have my full attention."

"Not even your clients?" I ask, aware that a little flirtation has slipped into my tone, but not quite able to squash it.

"That's strictly waist down," he says. "You're actually interesting."

He holds my gaze for a moment, and I feel a warmth traveling from my stomach to somewhere definitively lower. I break eye contact, glancing at the door.

"So, Lucifer's Ladies...black leather, lots of nose rings?"

"What?" Nico spins in his seat, suddenly alarmed. When

he turns back the muscles along his jawline are twitching, and I'm stifling laughter with my napkin.

"Sorry," I squeak. "It was too tempting."

The waiter comes with the check, and Nico intercepts me when I reach for it. "It's on me," he says.

"And so is a little bit of salsa," I tell him, leaning forward and swiping his lip with my napkin. He lets me, the tightness around his eyes softening a little.

Uncomfortable, I take another sip of the margarita. Despite my earlier protest, I've drunk more of it than I should, while Nico hasn't touched it at all. I push it toward him.

"You gotta help me finish this thing."

He reaches for the forgotten margarita, pulling it closer. "When the company is good, you don't need alcohol," he says, but even so he pulls the straw out and brings the glass up to his lips. But instead of drinking he frowns and then sniffs.

A minute later he's on his feet growling loud enough for everyone in the place to hear, "Who drugged my drink?"

14

I t turns out that Lucifer's Ladies really are a bunch of psychos. They seduced the bartender over a week ago and got him to promise he'd slip something into Nico's drink the next time he came by. It was just my luck that the next time was tonight. With me.

Also, that I was the only one to consume the drugged drink.

Except maybe it wasn't drugged, because I feel fine.

Sitting back in the booth, I watched as Nico shakes the bartender like a ragdoll. The bartender wets himself, which isn't pretty. But neither is drugging someone, so I didn't pity the dude. Eventually, Nico tires of his weeping and tosses him out into the alley with a warning that he should never let Nico see his face again. My money is on the guy getting on the first bus out of town. Nico then proceeds to rage at the restaurant staff as they in turn plead for his forgiveness. Nico isn't appeased until they promise him free food for life and that he can go behind the bar and make his own drinks whenever he wants.

Finally Nico turns back to me. Bracing both hands

against the tabletop, he leans in close, his one eye darting between both of mine. I realized he's trying to see if my pupils are dilated.

"I'm fine," I tell him.

"You think so?" he says, and then holds out a hand. I place mine into his, expecting him to help me up onto my feet. Instead, nerve endings I didn't even know I possessed light up all over my body. I gasp as all that feeling suddenly shifts, centering on what Mom used to refer to as my lady business. For example, "Paige, that skirt is so short I can almost see your lady business." Now my lady business is working overtime like a girl determined to break the glass ceiling once and for all. My internal muscles clench so hard that if there was a penis inside me right now, I'm pretty sure I'd pulp it.

Digging my nails into Nico's hand, I cry out and come. Right there, in the booth, in the middle of the Mexican restaurant.

Luckily, Nico's earlier outburst scared away the other patrons so no one is nearby to use the old, "I'll have what she's having" line.

Jerking away from Nico, I slide further back into the booth. "What the fuck?" I demand.

He takes his hand back. "It's a magical drug. Something made with incubus essence."

"Oh God, you mean sperm, don't you?" I moan. "I just drank sperm-flavored margarita."

Nico doesn't say anything, so I know I'm right.

"Look, I've used this drug before and it wears off pretty quickly," Nico says.

"How quickly?" I demand.

"A few hours."

I hold back a sob. "And what am I supposed to do until then?"

"You'll be fine as long as you don't touch anyone or anything living. It's touch that sets it off."

I swallow, as some of the panic recedes. "So I can just go home and sleep until it goes away?"

"Exactly."

"Great." Shooing Nico a good distance away, I slide out of the booth and dig into my purse for my car keys. That's when I remember. "My van is sentient. Does that count as living?" I close my eyes, fighting against a vision of my orgasming the whole way home. Even though it feels good, it also feels bad. Like my body's been hijacked. Also, I really think things would be weird between me and Vanna after a ride like that.

Nico frowns, considering the question. "I'll just have to drive you home," he says.

I sigh deeply. I really don't want to be anywhere near him right now, but there's no way around it.

"Okay, let's go."

Nico is careful to let me open my own door. He doesn't object either when I climb into the backseat, putting as much distance between us as I possibly can. I actually feel like I might get out of this whole thing without another embarrassingly public bone-shaking orgasm.

Then Nico pulls into my driveway and his headlights land on Brent standing on my front porch.

"Aw crap," I say.

"You want me to get rid of him?" Nico asks, a harsh growl in his voice.

"No," I say as I open my door and the car interior lights up. Brent's gaze lands on Nico and then me, in the backseat.

I watch as his expression tightens and then he strides toward us.

"Can you just not let him touch me?" I ask, desperate to not have to explain this whole thing to Brent. Where would I even start? 'So you know my ex-husband Jax, who you hate, and how he was accused of murder? Well I'm working with this werewolf to clear his name and while we had dinner I accidentally got drugged by a horny gang of biker bitches.'

Yeah, that's what I would say. And it would go over like a fart at a fancy dinner party.

I slide out of the car on the opposite side of Brent. Nico follows. Brent's eyes dart between us.

"What is this?" he demands.

"This is Nico..." I start to say.

Brent interrupts. "I know who it is."

Right. I forgot that he had my whole life investigated. I'm sure he knows all the tenants in the offices around mine. The fury I felt this morning ignites once more.

"Go away, Brent," I say. "I'm still pissed at you."

"And clearly you already have other plans for tonight," he sneers.

Brent starts to come around the car toward me, and Nico moves to cut him off, while saying in a calm voice, "We had a working dinner. Paige had a little too much to drink, so I drove her home. There's nothing else going on here."

"Whatever," Brent snarls and then he tries to push past Nico. But Nico doesn't move. They grapple for a moment and Brent must clearly realize that he's not going to win against Nico, because after a minute, he puts his hands up and backs away. "All right. You can have her," he says.

"Oh wow, noble."

Brent spins toward me. "What do you want from me,

Paige? I came here to talk. To patch things up and you come home with this guy!" He scrubs at his face. And when he looks at me again, the anger has given away to hurt. "Do you not care that I was going to propose this morning?"

Nico is quiet, but I can feel him beside me, absorbing this whole conversation. A conversation I really don't want to be having right now. But Brent deserves an answer.

I swallow and say softly. "I care."

It's true. I do. Even if I wouldn't have said yes, a proposal would've been nice. Brent has a future that's clearly going places. He could take any woman on that journey with him—maybe even Giselle, who has been beside him his entire career, supporting him and refreshing his coffee and rubbing his back. Okay, I don't know about the rubbing his back part. The ugly side of me is making that up. But Brent chose me. He proposed to *me*. And even if I'm undecided on whether or not I want that, it still feels good to be chosen.

I take a step closer to Brent, and farther from Nico. Away from the guy who led to my accidental drugging and toward the guy who represents stability and the wholesome sort of values that used to be considered a normal part of life.

Brent reaches into his pocket and I'm pretty sure it's for the ring. That he's gonna do the proposal right here, right now. And oh, I really don't want him to do that. But what he pulls out is even worse.

That damn supe stun gun again. And this time he's not playing around. He levels it straight at Nico and—

"No!" Without thinking, I launch myself sideways, spreading my body wide, trying to use my human self to block the blast.

Nico and I collide. My skin connecting with his at a thousand different points and that's before his arms close around me, pulling me close so that I don't slam to the ground.

My teeth rattle in my head. I don't just see stars. This orgasm brings whole galaxies to life. I am crying out with it and Brent is yelling my name and then the blast from the supe gun hits me. I thought humans were immune. But maybe because I'm touching Nico or maybe it's the incubus drug in my body confusing it. Whatever the reason, the gun stuns me, turning my whole body to ice.

The world in front of me grows dark at the edges, a sure sign that I'm about to pass out. But at least the orgasm has stopped. I feel nothing, every nerve ending in me is asleep or maybe even dead. At the moment, I don't really care which one.

"Paige, I'm sorry," I hear Brent say, but it's too late, I'm almost gone.

The last thing I say before I finally pass out is, "I think I just accidentally found a cure for the incubus sex drug."

15

I wake up in my bed and wonder who put me there.

I don't like the thought of either Nico or Brent carrying me into my bedroom. Brent because I'm still pissed at him for being a grade A a-hole, and Nico because the thought of him seeing where I sleep and do other bed things is a bit perverse.

I head downstairs and am not surprised to find Shauna at the table. What I am surprised at is a random woman puttering around the kitchen like she owns the place. She's singing to herself, a little ditty that she's clearly making up on the spot.

"Today we eat. We eat the meat. And ooh boy, it's gonna be sweet."

"What is happening?" I ask Shauna.

"Darron said something about you being sad you accidentally ate unicorn steaks, so he bought some real steaks for breakfast. I'm sad I missed the unicorn steaks though. They're so freaking good."

"They're really gross," I tell her. "Who is our guest?" This must be Darron's lady friend Jax mentioned when Darron first arrived—was that only a few mornings ago?

"This is Daphne. She's an absolute charm, and makes up lyrics on the spot! She can be a songwriter," Shauna says and looks fondly at Daphne's back.

I don't have the heart to tell her that Daphne's "lyrics" make me think more of Dr. Seuss than Bob Dylan. Daphne pivots and spins toward the fridge, grabbing a carton of eggs. Her full skirt flows around her with the move. She's giving off serious Donna Reed vibes. Did Darron nab a perfect housewife? Big skirt, apron, pearls.

"Is Darron joining us?" I ask.

Daphne turns and gives me a huge grin. "It's me or him, my dear. And I felt like dressing femme today!"

It takes me a second to realize what I'm seeing. Darron in a dress. He—she's beautiful. All the clothes make sense now, and Jax mentioning Darron's "lady friend" though he is clearly not over his wife's ghosting.

"Damn, girl," I say. "You got some nice legs."

"Isn't she just the best!?" Shauna shrieks. "So glamorous."

"Yes," I answer, watching Darron, I mean Daphne, finish cooking the eggs and plate them up. She puts a plate before me and one in front of Shauna, making sure the sugar bowl is within her reach.

Daphne sits, crosses her hands under her chin and gazes at me. "Questions?" she asks.

I blink. "Um...are you sure this isn't unicorn?" I ask. "I couldn't take my emotions being toyed with like that again."

She lets out a laugh. "USDA Grade A," she tells me. "I tried a bit while I was cooking. It's the real deal."

I can't believe I get to eat steak twice in one week. I take a bite and moan. "This is so good." I gulp some milky coffee and then shove in another helping. Okay, maybe having housemates isn't a total bust if they sometimes cook breakfast like Martha Stewart.

Daphne takes a small bite and chews daintily. "Any other questions?"

"What happened last night when I got home?"

"That bastard Brent shot you with a stun gun," Shauna tells me, ruining her steak by spooning sugar on top of it, then pouring pancake syrup over the whole mess. "Nico said you were drugged, I thought they were going to have a death match right on the lawn."

I shake my head. "Did anyone get hurt?"

"No, unfortunately Darron broke up the fight," Shauna tells me, not bothering to hide her disappointment.

"Brent left. Nico left. And we had to haul your heavy ass up the stairs. Maybe you should go on a diet..."

"Don't you finish that sentence," I tell Shauna, pointing my knife at her. "I won't be fat-shamed by a fae."

"I think you could actually put on a few pounds," Daphne tells me. "It doesn't hurt to have a little padding against the world." She cups her ample chest.

"Nico said to stop by his office," Shauna tells me. "He..." She puts down her fork. "He said he was sorry about Tina. I've heard stories about him being a bad guy, but he's really okay, I think."

"He's helping me find Kit's killer," I say.

"Any update?" she asks hopefully.

"I'm afraid not. Last night, I got, well, we got sidetracked."

She closes her eyes. "I'm trusting you to do this," she tells me. "You can't just 'get sidetracked'."

"I know, Shauna, I'm sorry, but I didn't exactly plan on being drugged. Today I am on the case, exclusively," I assure her. "And I will eat nothing that has not been prepared with my own two hands." Fork midway to my mouth with another bite of steak, I look at it and then to Shauna. "Or within this house," I quickly amend.

She nods, but doesn't look fully convinced or satisfied with my explanation. I'm not either, to be honest. I have three days left to get Jax out of jail, or lose my house to whatever kind of supe excels at poker. For some reason, I picture a manticore, and those claws are really going to scratch up my wood floors. Except they won't be mine anymore.

Realizing there's nothing I can say to make Shauna happy, I turn to Daphne. "I'm ready to ask those questions now if that's okay," I tell her with a smile.

She adjusts her pearls. "Go ahead, dear. I'm an open book."

"Are you trans...or are you..." I don't have the vocabulary, honestly.

"I'm not trans. I do dress in drag, though. You can call me he/him or she/her, and I won't be offended by either. I do like to go by Daphne when I'm dressed in women's clothes but if you slip up and call me Darron, I won't be mad." Daphne takes a small bite and continues.

"Drag started in the theatre, you know. During Shakespeare's time, all the actors were men. So some would have to dress as girls. It would be notated D-R-A-G. I always loved to dress up and I really love to try different costumes, transforming myself and playing a part." He tilts his head and smiles. "It makes me happy."

"Did your wife know?" I blurt out before realizing that might be a bit callous.

Daphne raises an eyebrow. "Dear, I may dress like a 1950s housewife on occasion, but this isn't the days of hiding in the closet. Of course, she knew. We loved each other and she was my best friend." He blinks hard and I'm afraid I got him ready to cry. "Sometimes she'd put on a tux and I'd get dolled up and we would go dancing."

"That sounds lovely," I tell him. And it does. I can't imagine someone loving me for all my quirks and imperfections, and me loving them for theirs.

I finish my breakfast and bring the plate to the sink. "Thank you for cooking," I tell Daphne. "Shauna, I think it's your job to do dishes."

She rolls her eyes but nods. "I guess since you're letting me stay here and finding Kit's killer and stuff," she agrees. "You are going to find him, right?" she asks.

"I'm on it," I assure her.

But first I need a shower. I start to head upstairs but Daphne cuts me off.

"It is okay, isn't it?" she asks, motioning up her body. "Some people are a bit uptight when they find out."

"Daphne or Darron, I really don't care. Unless you're a secret supe. For that I would have to kick you out," I tell her with a mischievous smile.

"Hey! I heard that!" Shauna calls from the other room. "You bigot."

I shake my head. How did I end up living with a mature drag queen and an immature fae girl?

16

I have a few missed calls from Brent, which I ignore, and a few more from Nico. I don't want to face either of them, and debate just checking out the rest of the leads by myself, but Nico knows more about the supe's world than I do, so I give in and call him.

"Paige! Are you okay? I'm sorry about the drink. I had no idea…"

"It's fine," I tell him. "It's not your fault."

"I should have protected you."

Whoa, hold up. "Look, I get you're an alpha, big bad werewolf, but I'm not yours to protect. Got it?"

He actually growls, his guttural sound coming through my phone. "Fine. I get it."

"I'm going to the warehouse now. Meet me there. Or don't. It's up to you." I hang up the phone frustrated. Nico is so very infuriating.

I head outside to find Vanna drove herself home last night. I've never been so happy to have a sentient vehicle. I plug the address into my GPS and then roll out. My phone rings again and I roll my eyes. Fuck Brent. Fuck Nico.

But it's a number I don't recognize. Might be a client. I really could use the money. I push the hands-free button.

"You are receiving a collect call from an inmate at a New Jersey correctional facility. Do you accept the charges?"

"Yes!" I shout.

There's a click, then Jax's voice says, "Hey babe."

"Not your babe," I tell him.

"You sound weird. Are you in the car?" he asks, his voice small. Honestly, he's the one that sounds weird...kind of low energy. I guess jail will do that to even the most charismatic guy.

"Yeah, driving to a place where hopefully I'll find a murderer." Argh, that sounds bad even to my ears.

"It's too dangerous," Jax tells me. "Please. Just go back home."

"What are you talking about?" I say, my eyes on the road. "You're in jail. Right now. We have to get you out and get my house back."

"The house...right..." Jax goes quiet and I think he's hung up. But then he says, "A house is just a place. You can get a new house. A better one."

"I love that house," I tell him. "What's going on?"

"Nothing. Just be careful. It's not worth your life," he says.

"Jax, stop the shit. What's wrong?" I'm starting to worry. "Are the vamps hassling you? I thought you were protected by those pixie guys."

"I am. It's just... It's not worth it. Not if you get hurt. I can't protect you from inside here." Not this shit again.

"I can protect myself," I yell. "I don't need you, or Nico..."

"Who?"

I let out a frustrated huff. "Just keep your head down. I'm clearing your name. End of story..."

"Please be careful," he tells me and his voice is so earnest my stomach drops.

"You too," I say as I pull into the warehouse parking lot. "Gotta go."

"I love you, Paige," he says before the line goes dead.

I shake my head and swallow hard. WTF, Jax?

Getting out of the van, I notice there's a ton of cars, maybe workers at the warehouse? There's a line formed along the wall and it looks like a bouncer situation at the door. People are dressed oddly, like it's steampunk night at a club. The women are all wearing corsets and petticoats and the men are in suits and top hats.

I try to get a look inside but get yelled at for cutting the line. I spot Nico a few people in and elbow my way to him. "I'm with him!" I tell a pale girl in a black Victorian gown.

"Oh, now you need me?" he asks.

I roll my eyes. "What is going on here?"

"My guess?" he whispers. "Themed straw party. Vamp groupies love a good Dracula moment."

"We are severely underdressed," I say.

"That won't be our only problem," he replies and motions to the person standing next to the bouncer, a bored girl, maybe twenty, in a very modern-looking rainbow-colored Love is Love T-shirt.

The bouncer is a big guy, all muscle and menace. But he defers to the small girl with the rainbow T-shirt. Clearly, she's calling the shots.

The couple in front of us are answering questions from the bouncer. I catch the guy saying, "I've only eaten honey for the last three days."

The bouncer looks to the girl in the rainbow tee and she nods.

Addressing the couple again, the bouncer asks, "Take any ibuprofen or blood thinners?"

"No," the couple answer in unison.

The bouncer once more looks to the girl. This time instead of a nod, she simply sighs. "The girl is lying.".

"No, I mean...I took some Midol last week but..."

"You're out," the bouncer tells her.

Nico moves in and whispers in my ear, "The one next to the bouncer is a witch. Some kind of lie detector spell."

The bouncer turns to the guy. "You can go in solo or stay with your girlfriend. Leave your phone at check in, then proceed to the right."

The guy doesn't even hesitate, he goes through the door, leaving the girl to huff and puff.

"Harsh," I mutter as we step up.

The bouncer looks at us and says, "Nope. Next!"

"Hey!" I say. "I may not look like an Interview with a Vampire reject but...I've eaten steak two days in a row. That's gotta be worth something."

The girl puts a hand on the bouncer's arm and he immediately loses the attitude. "Have you taken any blood thinners or ibuprofen?" he asks. Nico and I both answer no.

"Are you both human?"

I say yes, but Nico doesn't say anything. Shit. For a second I forgot that he *isn't* human.

"I'm a werewolf," Nico says.

The bouncer shakes his head. "No werewolves. You got a set of balls on you, though. Coming here." He turns to me. "You can go in without him."

"Hold on," Nico says. "She'll be right back." Without asking my opinion, Nico wraps his hand around my upper arm and pulls me a few feet away.

"Are you sure you want to go in there alone?" he asks.

"Yes! I have three days left to free Jax and get him to that poker game. Otherwise I'm out on my ass. And Jax will be stuck in prison..." I trail off lamely. Nico doesn't comment on my messed up priorities. Instead, he begins to unbutton my shirt.

"What are you doing?" I demand.

"Helping you," he replies tersely as he continues to flick buttons open one by one. I slap at his hands, but he keeps going. One button. Then two. And three. Until half my bra is exposed.

The demure button-up I'd chosen this morning after waking up and still not feeling quite safe exposing my skin, is suddenly a lot more risqué.

"Excuse you," I say. "I don't—"

But Nico isn't done. He puts one hand on my shoulder and another on my elbow. And then gives one sharp jerk. The seam at the top of my arm gives away. He repeats the same maneuver on my other arm. The fabric slides down, bunching at my wrists.

"Hey," I protest. "This is my nice shirt! I mean, I got it off the clearance rack at Dress Barn, but still." Ignoring me, Nico continues his work. I sigh, giving in. "You wanna at least tell me why I'm being subjected to Nico's superfast alterations?"

He flashes me a quick grin, but then his face grows serious once more. One of his long fingers traces across the inside of my wrist and then up to the crook of my elbow, running along the blue trails of my veins. "The people inside don't care about dress up bullshit. That's just something to keep their guests entertained. This is what they want to see." His hands moves and now his touch moves to my neck and down over my collar bone. "If you want to ask questions, you need to get close. And..." His fingers dip right into the depths of my cleavage and snaps something onto the middle bit of my bra.

"It's a camera, right?" I say, pretending to be unmoved by his touch, even though I'm struggling to keep my breath even. "And here I was thinking you were just some creep trying to cop a feel."

Nico's eyes twinkle. "Oh, I'm definitely that too."

I can't help but laugh because he is without shame. "You'll be watching?" I ask, getting us back on track.

"And listening," Nico says. He holds out a small black earpiece, "Can you wear your hair down on one side to hide this? That way I can talk to you too. Warn you away from anyone too dangerous."

I don't know how I feel about Nico watching the party from my cleavage and then ordering me around, but I also don't like the idea of going in there alone. With a sigh, I rearrange my hair and take the earpiece from his hand. Nico makes me wait another minute while he pulls out his phone and tests to make sure everything works. After that, there's no other reason to stall.

But I do, for just a minute. I allow myself a breath.

"You don't have to do this," Nico says. "It's probably a dead end. Kit was a vampire. He was feeding."

"We don't know that for sure," I say. "Not until I go in there and find out."

Straightening my shoulders, I head back toward the bouncer and the truth witch. Despite my bravado, my legs wobble a little beneath me. I'm heading into a vampire party, not as the cleanup crew, but as the main dish.

17

I was expecting some type of old-timey party inside. Instead, as my eyes adjust to the darkness within, I realize I've entered the jungle. Trees and giant potted plants fill the space around me. Somewhere deeper inside a low drumbeat sounds, building the tension deep within my belly. Between beats, distant shrieks and giggles mix with the rustling of leaves.

The entire effect is so overwhelming that I take a step back and walk right into the couple coming in behind me.

He's dressed in one of those round explorer hard hats. She has on a long white dress with binoculars strung around her neck.

"My gawd, the new world," she says, looking around, her accent a mix of Jersey and a not very convincing British.

"By jove, it is," the man agrees. "I do hope the natives aren't restless."

They both giggle at this and then without any further talk, push their way into the greenery and disappear.

It occurs to me I might be the only sane person in this whole building. It is not a comforting thought.

"Wonder who's getting paid to clean up this mess?" Nico says in my ear.

I'd forgotten he was there, watching from between my boobs. Now I cling to his voice. And his words.

Because he's right. Someone will have to clean up this mess. And they didn't book me. I tilt my head back to study the ceiling. Tree limbs are bolted to it with thick wire cables, just barely disguised with lots of drapey moss. Someone will have to get up there with a cherry picker and some bolt cutters. But that won't be the worst part of this job. They must have hauled in a few tons of dirt to cover this floor.

Cleaning this all up would be a two-day job at least. And I'd charge extra for hazard pay, because who knows what creepy crawlies might be hiding in all this greenery. Now I'm actually bummed they didn't call me.

"Feeling okay?" Nico asks, his voice low and uncomfortably intimate in my ear. Maybe because it seems like he's more than just in my ear; he seems to have somehow crawled into my head as well.

"I'm fine," I say in a low undertone. "Just getting my bearings."

Wishing I'd brought a machete, I duck beneath a low tree branch and find my way into the forest. I immediately spot a woman in a big floofy dress, tied to a tree. Several vamps are around her, using their straws to sample blood that drips down her neck and arms. My first instinct is to shoo the vamps away and then get her down. But I doubt she'd thank me for that. A smile of pure bliss covers her face.

Okay, then. Different strokes for different folks, I guess.

Turning on my heel, I head in another direction.

"Paige, stop marching around aimlessly," Nico says. "And

get that 'look at me the wrong way and I'll neuter you' look off your face," he adds.

"You can't see my face."

Nico snorts. "I don't have to. Anytime you're within ten feet of a supe that's the look you have on your face."

"You're wrong," I counter. "That's a special look I save only for you," I murmur sweetly.

"Yeah?" Nico laughs, low and sultry. "Your boyfriend Brent would say otherwise."

"Shut up," I hiss, not wanting to hear any more of Nico's thoughts about my relationship with Brent.

But he is right about me not making an attractive target.

I shake out my hands which have been balled into fists. Then finding a wide tree trunk, I lean against it, fling an arm over my forehead and declare, "Oh dear me, I am a rare and delicate flower, lost and alone in a strange place. Surely a strong man will come and save me."

"Rare and delicate flower, my ass," Nico snorts in my ear.

And that's it. I've had enough of his commentary for now. Plucking his earpiece out, I drop it into the dirt at my feet and then give it a good stomp, driving it into the soft dirt beneath my feet.

"Ahem," someone says from behind me.

I tense, ready to fight, and then remember that I'm here to play nice and get information. But when I turn it's a man in a three-piece suit who looks just as out of place as me.

"Stranger in a strange land?" he asks, his English accent is perfect. I can't tell if it's real or not.

I don't even attempt to match him there and just stick with my normal Jersey sound. "Yep. I've never been bit."

"Ah," he leans in closer and lowers his voice. "If you want more attention, your virgin status will gain many admirers."

"Yeah…" I shake my head. "I'm not really sure about this whole thing yet, so I'd rather keep that under my hat for now." I study the guy. He looks unrumpled and there's not a streak of blood on him. "What about you?" I ask him. "You come here a lot?"

"Unfortunately." He reaches into his suit jacket and extracts a card.

Dark Side Tours, it reads. "We safely guide you through the underbelly of the supernatural world."

"Nice," I say as I dig into my back pocket for one of my own cards.

Taking it, he reads it and then smiles. "Seems like we've both found ways to deal with life's lemons."

I smile, liking him. He's handsome in his suit. Neatly groomed too. Nothing flashy about him, but there's an intelligence in his eyes. You don't find that last bit in every good-looking guy.

"Paige," I say, holding out my hand.

"Liam," he answers, taking my hand and clasping it within both of his. "Pleased to make your acquaintance."

He doesn't release me but the moment feels warm rather than overpowering. We smile at each other.

Meanwhile, I can almost sense Nico outside having a fit that I'm chatting with this guy instead of finding a vamp to pump for answers while he pumps precious O negative out of my veins.

Then I realize, if Liam comes here a lot, maybe he saw Kit.

"Look," I say, edging in a bit closer to him. "The truth is I'm also here for business instead of pleasure." My phone was held at check-in so I don't have that to show him Kit's pic. But maybe a name and description. "I'm looking for someone. This was one of the last places he was seen before he died."

"The vamps in charge won't like that." Liam frowns. "They won't want it to get out that their blood supply might endanger themselves by coming here."

"No, no." I shake my head. "It was a vamp that was killed. He died from blood thinners and stab wounds. It looked like the vamp serial killer—"

Liam's hand came down on my arm. "Do not mention that around here if you value your life. The vamps are in denial that the hunters have turned prey."

I frown at that. "I don't think they're in complete denial. They've hired a PI to look into it—"

Liam's eyebrows rise at this and then he shakes his head ruefully. "Perhaps my sources are not what I was led to believe. I try to keep the inside track on all things supernatural in order to keep my clients safe. But as a human..." He shrugs. "Sometimes I think they misinform me just for fun."

I nod at this. "Count on it. Especially if you ever use a fae as an informant. I wouldn't trust one of them for directions to cross the street."

"Right." He nods. "I've heard that—"

A vampire drops down in front of us as if he just fell from the sky. His black hair is slicked back and he rocks an ebony bat necklace, the two eyes studded with diamonds. Well, there's no accounting for taste. Crouched in front of me, he flashes his fangs. "I claim you," he says, brandishing a fancy black straw, also studded with diamonds.

"Ugh, no thanks," I say, trying to back away, but not having anywhere to go with the tree behind me.

The vamp smiles, showing off red-stained teeth and lips. I've looked that way after I've hit the red wine too hard. But I know it's not vino that he's been sucking down.

Liam steps in between us. "Sorry," he says to the vamp. "She's one of mine. A party pooper. I was just going to escort her back out to the van."

The vamp hisses softly and reaches around Liam to snag my wrist. His fingernail rakes across it, drawing blood. "A party favor," he says, and then licks the blood from the tip of his finger.

"You're violating the rules," Liam says, his voice fierce and strong and certain.

The vamp rolls his eyes, like Liam is his uptight dad. "Whatever," he answers, but with a leap, he disappears from view once more.

Feeling woozy, I cover the wound on my wrist, trying to staunch the bleeding. Liam turns to me, concern on his face...

And fangs in his mouth.

18

I shove Liam away, furious with him.

"Wait," he protests. He reaches a hand into his mouth and pops the fangs out.

My eyes go wide as he holds them on the middle of his palm.

"Fakes," he explains. "Humans like the idea of a tamed vampire. The vamps mostly aren't fooled, except ones that like that are so full of blood they're seeing everything through a pink haze."

"I'm impressed," I say. And I am.

Liam is like me, making his living by walking among supes that could literally crush us on a whim. We've both had to be savvier and stronger than the rest of our kind to survive.

I feel like I've found a kindred spirit.

"Let me get you out of here," Liam says. "I know you're looking for answers, but the vamps aren't going to help a human. Once you start asking questions, they'll show you the door."

I don't protest as Liam's hand lands on my lower back

and he begins to guide me out of the maze of trees and shrubbery.

"What about you?" I ask. "Maybe we could meet up sometime? I could show you pics of Kit—that's the dead vamp. It's possible you've seen him around…"

We've reached the door, but Liam doesn't reach for the handle. "I love the meet up idea. Although, I must admit, I was hoping to make it more of a date."

"Oh," I say, blushing a little. "I'm sort of seeing someone at the moment…"

The truth is Liam is pretty much my idea of the perfect guy. But at the same time, between Nico, Jax, and Brent I'm juggling a lot of male attention right now. Maybe, though, Liam is different.

"Of course." Liam nods. "I apologize."

He grabs the door handle and I place my hand over his.

"But," I add, "we're having a rough patch. More than that, really. The thing is—"

Liam cuts me off, gently, with a touch of his hand to my cheek. "I understand completely. Why don't you text me the pictures from your dead vamp and I'll let you know if I recognize him. I'll even reach out to some of my colleagues. And if your relationship status changes…call me."

I grin. "Perfect."

I slip out the door into the bright sunshine of a beautiful day. The inside of the fake jungle was cold, but I don't need the sun to warm me. Liam already did that.

Laughing a little at myself, I realize what just happened.

For the first time in ages I met a nice normal guy. And it only took going to a vampire straw party for it to happen.

———

Nico is a bit mad that I ditched the earpiece (and left it at the straw party) but when I promise to reimburse him he drops it. I tell Vanna to head home and let Nico drive to the next address.

"I thought the straw party would be a bust," Nico mutters. Reaching into the glove compartment he pulls out a first aid kit and tosses me a bandage for my wrist.

"Not completely," I say, thinking of Liam.

"What?" Nico asks, eyeing me suspiciously.

"Nothing...I just realize I must have competition in the supernatural clean-up game." I spread some antiseptic ointment on my wound and wrap the bandage around my wrist. I better not get some vamp STD or something from this. Maybe I can sue that vamp—I wonder if his bling was real. "That's why my business has dried up. I don't know why I haven't heard anything about it."

"If it's a supe, you wouldn't."

I shake my head. "A supe is taking my work?!"

"Don't give me the supes are stealing our jobs speech, Paige. I'm not in the mood."

I roll my eyes. "I'm not actually a bigot," I say. "But..."

"Just leave it at that, I think," Nico says with a sigh. And I do. More to avoid a fight then to appease Nico.

We pull up in front of a house and Nico motions to the one across the street. No car in the driveway. No lights on. It looks pretty deserted.

"How do you feel about a little B&E?" Nico asks.

"A *little* breaking and entering?" I say. "I feel like that's something you either do, or you don't. Like you can't be *kind of* pregnant."

Nico gives me a smile that makes me want to amend that last statement. I feel kind of pregnant right now. Who knows what else was laced in that margarita? I might be super fertile and just being in the proximity of sex appeal could knock me up.

"I've got three days to figure this out, so I'm game," I say. "But if we get caught..."

"You're my prisoner," he says. "Under a control spell that makes you incapable of denying me."

"That's kind of you to fall on your sword like that," I tell him, suspiciously.

"It's not kindness, it's practicality. There's no reason for us both to go down." He actually blushes a bit, then continues, "and people will believe anything of a supe. You're just a poor defenseless human girl. Hence the mind control spell."

"Um...before we get out of the car you need to tell me that is not an actual thing."

"Oh, it's a thing," Nico says, popping his door open. "It's considered very dark magic in the supe world, and it's rarely used for B&E's."

"I bet," I mutter, following him out onto the street. Surprisingly, he takes my hand, interlacing his fingers with mine. I try to pull back, but he squeezes.

"We're a couple," he says. "Out for a walk. We're very much in love and we're visiting our friend, who just went through a breakup."

I put an elbow into his side and pull my hand away. "We're a couple," I agree, "but sadly we're no longer very much in love. In fact, we're on our way to a very private, very high-end therapist to find out if there's a way to fix this relationship."

"Hmm," Nico says in a low laughing voice. "That's right. I asked the doctor if he could squeeze us in today for a special appointment. I just want to know why my wife says the spark is gone, when I can still make her come with only the touch of my hand."

I glare at Nico and hiss in a low voice, "It doesn't count if I'm drugged!"

"Easy." He puts his hands up. "I didn't mean the other night. I just meant..." He grins in that way he has like he knows he's irresistible. "I'm very good with my hands."

"Gross," I say with an eye roll. I'm lucky the little lie detector witch isn't anywhere nearby or she'd call me out in two seconds, because the idea of how good Nico might be with his hands is enough to—

No. I'm not going there. Between Jax and Brent I've got enough man troubles. I don't need to throw Nico into the mix.

"Backstory. I own a high-end pet obedience training center," I say as we cross the street to the house. "I strictly deal in exotic crossbreeds, like Dalmanthers."

Dalmanthers are an amazingly sleek new domestic animal that the world was gifted after a panther shifter got kinky with a Dalmatian. They're a type of spotted cog (cat/dog) with fierce loyalty and a prey drive from hell. Last month a woman's Dalmanther ate her three Corgis. Apparently, she showed a little too much affection to the little dogs and the Dalmanther decided to take out the competition.

"Obedience, huh?" Nico's eyebrows raise. "Okay. And we worked together at the Westminster Dog Show. I needed an extra hand on my—"

"Easy, buddy," I interject.

"I was going to say Golden Retriever." The look he gives me is as guileless and sweet as a puppy. I'm not fooled for a minute.

"A Golden Retriever, huh?" I snort. "Would've thought you'd go for something with a little more flash."

"I have nothing against domestication," Nico says as we climb the steps to the front porch. "You'd be surprised how much I have in common with a Golden."

"I didn't peg you for a shedder," I say, and he lets go of my hand to knock on the door. The sound reverberates through the house, but no movement follows. Nico shades his eyes and peers in through the glass cutout.

"No, but we're both very stubborn, we won't be deterred if we want something, and"—he turns to me, a small curl at the side of his mouth—"we need a lot of vigorous exercise."

"Is that a fact?" I ask, stepping back from him and casually tossing my hair over my shoulder, taking a glance through a window at the same time. "I guess I'm more like a terrier, then."

"How's that?" Nico asks

"Once I get my mouth on something, I won't let go," I tell him, arching one eyebrow.

He emits another low growl, and takes my hand, urging me off the porch and into the dark. I'm pretty sure we're still *investigating* and not *foreplaying*, but I let go of his hand, just in case.

"Nobody's home," he says, his voice now cool and collected, his face in shadow. "I'll climb the fence and go around back. Stay at the front door, and if anybody comes along and questions you—"

"I'm a Census taker," I say.

Nico's one eye passes over me. "More like a high-class hooker."

I give him a warning glare. "You're the one who ripped my clothes!"

"Don't be mad. I said, high-class." He turns and jogs to the side of the house.

I try not to be impressed when Nico scales the fence in

one leap. Soon I hear him moving through the house, and see a penlight come on inside. There's a rustling as he unlocks the door, and I slip past him into a surprisingly spare front hall.

The front lawn was immaculate, with the added touch of flower boxes in front of the windows. Everything outside was arranged in a welcoming, suburban method—you can come here, but only if you compliment my taste first.

But the interior is something completely different. Nico's penlight moves over bare walls as we proceed further into the house. And I pull out my own phone and flip on the flashlight app. An empty hallway leads to bedrooms without beds—or furniture of any kind.

"You say Kit spent the night here?" Nico asks.

"According to the tracker app," I answer, pulling open a closet to find empty wire hangers.

"Nothing," I say. "Nobody lives here."

Nico's light sweeps the small interior of the closet, and a flash at my feet catches my eye.

"Wait," I say, motioning to the floor. "Look."

There's a pair of shiny silver handcuffs.

"Nobody lives here," Nico says, examining the inside of the closet doors, where there are scuff marks. "But someone was kept here."

We both hear a footstep in the hallway a second too late, our eyes widening as the hall light comes on. Nico pushes me into the closet, following close behind as he pulls the door closed. It's a tight fit. Nico is a big guy, and my face is buried in his chest.

The footsteps pass by our room, and a second later, the hall light goes off. We both exhale in relief, his breath warm against my face.

"I've got my gun," I whisper to him, and his fingers trace

the small of my back. I'm about to object when they find the weapon tucked into my pants.

"Human gun," he says. "That's good. You'll have us covered on that end."

"You have a supe gun?" I ask, returning the favor as I let my fingers run the width of his waistband. He inhales sharply, and it becomes apparent that he is, in fact, packing.

"Oh," I say in mock surprise. "I think you brought two."

"Paige," he growls in warning, but his hands tighten against my waist and he pulls me against him. I can feel his stubble on my forehead and I know that if I just turn my head and look up we will have crossed a line from working together to...something else entirely.

I push my hands against his chest, separating our bodies just the tiniest bit. "Let's stop it there," I whisper. "We both got a feel in. Now let's be adults and keep our hands to ourselves."

"Right," Nico answers, his voice cold even at its low volume. "Although, let me be clear that my definition of adulthood is not about keeping my hands to myself."

"Clearly," I can't resist sniping back at him.

"For someone who dresses the way you do," Nico hisses back. "You sure can be a prude."

"What the hell is that supposed to mean?"

"It means that if you're going to rub up against me—"

Exasperated I shove him. "You pulled me in here!" My voice rises above a whisper, but I can't say that I care that much anymore. Or that I'm even thinking about anything other than putting more space between myself and Nico. I shove him again, fairly certain there's more room in this closet and he's just crowding me for effect.

Or maybe not. I bang against the door behind me and it must not have been latched securely because it swings open.

Feeling myself falling, I reach out blindly, and get a handful of Nico's shirt.

"Ah, hair!" he growls. Oops. And some chest hair too.

We land in a heap on the floor, Nico landing half on top of me.

"Augh, get off," I say as softly as possible, although at this point it's safe to say our presence has probably been detected. The thud we made was loud enough to shake the whole house.

I roll away from Nico, ready to jump to my feet and face whatever danger is coming at us. But Nico has other thoughts.

"Wait," he commands. His hand comes down on the middle of my back, pushing me into the ground. I wriggle but he just applies more force.

I turn my head so I can at least see him. His gaze is focused on the door and his nose is in the air, sniffing.

"What?" I demand, hating that he has these extra senses and extra strength at his disposal, while my only move is to kick my legs and have a very human temper tantrum.

Nico suddenly goes tense. Then he springs to his feet, releasing me.

Two seconds later, a blood-curdling scream erupts from the other room.

19

Nico bursts into the kitchen, with me hot on his heels, to find Kirkland pinned to the wall, a pixie fist in his face.

"Shauna!" I yell, and she spins toward me, but the fist doesn't go down. Kirkland makes a move for the back door but Nico is faster, intercepting him with a snarl that reminds me he's a supe, and capable of turning into a bloodthirsty monster at any time.

"Did you really think you were going to do this without me?" Shauna shrieks in my face, her rage honing in on a new target.

"You followed us," I say, eyes narrowing.

"I can use the app too, dummy," she huffs, then glances over at Nico. "Hey man."

"Hey Shauna," he says, eyes still on Kirkland, who is sizing up each of us and weighing his options.

"Listen," Kirkland says smoothly, locking in on me. "I think we need to have a talk. Whatever it is you think—"

He doesn't get a chance to finish. There's a *Boom* as Shauna slips into pixie form, and a high hum in the air as she spins in tight circles, moving so fast she's a blur. I'm mesmerized, pulled in by the sparks flying off her.

"Paige! Get down!" Nico bellows at me, and I hit the floor. I have no idea what's going on, but the last time I ignored a warning from Nico I almost had my head torn off by a harpy on meth.

Being fae himself, Kirkland knows what's about to happen, but instinct prevails and he puts his hands out to protect himself—just as Shauna spins out of her loop, her tiny body now a projectile as she zooms straight though his palm.

Kirkland screams, and I can see his mouth stretched wide through the perfectly round hole in the middle of his hand. His pinkie barely dangles from a string as Shauna snaps back into human size, blood spatter in her hair.

"You fuck with me, you're going to need both hands," she menaces, vampire fangs erupting.

"Stop!" I yell, stepping in between the two of them. She hisses at me, flashing her fangs and dancing back and forth, as if about to pounce. "We need him," I remind her. "If you want to know what happened to Kit, we've got to get him to talk."

"I know what happened to him! He was killed! Now the only thing left is to make this mofo pay." There are at least twenty kinds of crazy in Shauna's eyes. Which is about eight more than usual.

Anyone else would run. But I love my house. And I guess there are enough feelings left in my heart for Jax that I don't want him to go down for a crime he didn't commit.

So I try to put myself in Shauna's tiny little shoes. Her brother was murdered. He was the last person left in her life. Her wife disappeared. She's pissed off all her friends so many times that they've lost her number. The only thing she has to look forward to in her life is getting revenge on her brother's killer.

Okay, I can work with that.

"Shauna, listen," I say, snapping my fingers in front of her face.

She doesn't even blink. I might as well not even be standing here.

Nico comes up beside me. He takes the penlight he had earlier and sweeps it across her face and then up to the ceiling. Her eyes follow it. Nico turns the light so it's in my eyes. I put a hand up so it's not blinding me. Nico knocks my hand away.

"She's watching you now, so talk," he says.

Oh right. Fae have this thing for light. And shiny objects. When I was married to Jax I thought he had some sort of undiagnosed brain injury because of the way he'd become attracted to lights. Especially at Christmas time. We once went to an outdoor Festival of Lights thing and he refused to leave until the place closed and they turned the lights out.

"Shauna," I say, knowing I have her attention as long as Nico's light is directing her attention to me. I appeal to her the only way I know how. "I know you want to end the guy who killed Nico. But we don't know if he did it. We just know he was part of what happened. But there might be others out there who had a hand in Kit's death. Do you want them to get away with it?"

"No," Shauna says softly.

"Then we gotta get more out of good old Kirkland here than just screams of pain."

"I want him to suffer," Shauna says.

"I know," I say gently.

The light in my eyes suddenly goes out. I blink as white

blobs fill my vision. When I can focus again, I see Shauna still looking steadily at me. Which means, I've got her.

"Can't I at least make him beg more?" she asks, fangs disappearing into an adorable pout.

God, supes. How is this my life?

"Please," Kirkland's voice comes from behind me, high and pleading. "She's a crazy bitch! You've got to help me."

"Help you?" I spin on my heel to face him. I can't make my body into a missile, or suddenly morph into a wolf, but I was raised in Jersey, and appealing to my better side isn't going to get this supe freak anywhere.

"Help you?" I repeat, outrage rising. "You hired me under false pretenses, lured me to a murder scene, and then framed my ex. The only thing I'm going to help you do is become a eunuch, and I do think it's possible to separate the scrotum from the male body with bare hands."

"It is," Nico confirms.

"But unlike my sister-in-law—who you called a crazy bitch, and you *will* be apologizing for that—I can be persuaded away from violence."

I tap one fingernail against Kirkland's nose and a high whine escapes him as he presses against the wall with nowhere to go.

"You can talk to me back in my office, or I can leave you with these two. Your call."

Kirkland swallows once, a dry click in his throat. He's cradling his mangled hand to his chest, and blood has seeped down his shirt onto his pants. He's cornered and injured, and while supes might be superhuman, they're still animals, and an animal knows when it's caught.

"Alright," Kirkland says. "I'll talk."

———

Kirkland's willingness to cooperate evaporates once we get to my office. I called Darron to come collect Shauna and sent them home with stern instructions not to come back, and the combination code to the safe I lock all my sweets in. Some people have a cookie jar, but once I married Jax it became clear that a cookie safe was the better choice for our home. Even after he left, I kept using it out of habit.

Shauna's not going to be happy when she gets home and discovers there's more ammunition than AirHeads in there, but hopefully we'll have gotten something useful from Kirkland by then.

"Okay," I say, sitting down across from Kirkland. We're in the back room of my office, bottles of bleach and fresh mop heads stacked high around us. There's not a lot of space. We barely squeezed in two folding chairs, and my knees are still touching his. I wonder briefly if I should have done the whole sit-on-the-chair-backwards thing, complete with manspread.

"You said you would talk," I remind Kirkland. "Talk."

He smiles at me, lifts his bloodied hand, which I had quickly wrapped in cleaning rags as soon as we arrived. "Might not have been a good move, ditching your tiny torture device so quickly," he says.

"I've still got him," I say, jerking my head behind me to where Nico stands, back against the door.

"Oh, so is this good cop, bad cop? Or wait..." He lifts his bandaged hand, "Sexy nurse, grumpy doctor? I could get into that. What do you say, Paige? Need a little supe sex in your life? Or how about a lot?"

I smile, lean forward. "You forget, I was married to a fae. I know your tricks. I know how you manipulate conversations, changing the subject until I forget the point. But not this time. Not with Jax in jail and my house on the line."

"Your house?" Kirkland asks, real confusion on his face.

"And as for the sex...I hear fae are the least endowed of the supes."

It's a low blow, and also—if Jax is any indication—definitely untrue, but a groin shot, real or metaphorical, is always a great starting point. As expected, the faux smile fades from Kirkland's face, but it's rage burning there, not resignation. He leans forward, his breath sickly sweet.

"Listen to me, you little human bitch," he says, a snarl curling his lip. "You don't know who you're messing with. If you've got a sliver of common sense, you'll drop this. Go home. Curl up with your Humans First boy toy and forget that this ever happened."

My hackles rise. Has he been watching me? Kirkland's eyes stay on mine, following my thoughts.

"Me? Follow you?" He chuckles. "No dear, sorry. Not interested. But I do have a team at my disposal, and if you think it's only me you have to worry about, you are in so far over your head that Wilson Phillips couldn't save you."

I snort, then clap a hand over my mouth. "Sorry, sorry," I say. "It's just...you were doing so good. You had the threatening tone." I lower my voice, make it gravelly. "You were working on a great glower." I turn my mouth upside down, push my eyebrows together. "And your threats, they were decent. But then you slipped up and blew everything out of the water...you see what I did there?"

I smile at him, and his mouth goes into a straight line.

"Faerieland Faes," I say, shaking my head. "You haven't been here long enough to make pop culture references. You were trying to say I was in such deep water that Michael

Phelps couldn't save me, but you swapped out an Olympian for an 80s pop band. That's a bad look."

Kirkland pulls back, sits straighter, tries to gather some dignity.

"Nico," I call over my shoulder. "Could you go into the front office and bring Vee in here, please?"

He tilts his head. "Vee? The plant?"

I nod.

The door clicks closed behind me, and I cross my legs, keeping an eye on Kirkland.

"You threatened me, and I didn't like that," I tell him. "I'm going to let you think about that, here in this very small room, overnight. And my friend Vee will be joining you. She's a sentient Venus fly trap. I haven't fed her in a few days, and us dirty humans aren't the only ones who like a little bit of meat in their diet."

The door opens and there's a clink as Nico sets Vee's potting jar on the floor. She immediately tips it, crawling forward on her leaves, massive head swiveling as she tries to locate the smell of the blood. Kirkland leaps out of his chair, perching on the edge and holding his arm above his head.

"Please, wait..." he says. "I'll talk."

"You already said that once," I tell him, folding my chair and propping it against the wall. Vee pulls herself into an upright position, scenting the air. "Hopefully this time you mean it," I say, flicking off the storage room light.

"I'll check in tomorrow to see where you landed on that," I say, before closing the door. I half-sing my final line to him, even though I'm fairly sure it'll go right over his head.

"I can hold on for one more day."

20

I drop Nico off at his apartment, which is in a much nicer neighborhood than my house. He opens his door, then pauses.

"You going to be okay for tonight?" he asks.

"Offering to keep me company?" I say, pulling my gaze from the rearview mirror. I mean, Nico is hot, but I am exhausted. The only thing that has my full attention right now is the thought of my own bed—and I intend to be alone in it.

Before he can answer I say dismissively, "Yeah, I'm fine. I regularly threaten supes and leave them tied up in the back room overnight."

Nico gives me a hard stare. "I believe you."

I smack his shoulder, annoyed that I'm smiling. "Get out of my van"

He does, but taps the roof before I drive away. "Call me if you need me," he says, and I pull away so fast I hope that it communicates that I don't, in fact, need him at all. I also hope it does *not* convey that I was sort of re-thinking it there for a second, and stamp on the gas to make a quick getaway from any more bad decisions on my part.

I drive home in a pensive state. Jax told me he still loves me, Brent wants to marry me (at least, I think he still does), Nico's body has made it clear he doesn't mind being near me, and the Liam guy from the straw party keeps running through my mind.

He was so...normal. So...human. And not human like Brent, who can be a total animal in bed and then a housecat in public; somebody you'd hand your baby *to*, not make a baby *with*.

It's given me pause, more than once, the way Brent can switch over from being his public self to his private self. I know that's part of the game he plays—and plays well. But part of me isn't quite sure that a guy who is able to turn the tables that quickly can be totally trusted. I'd asked him once which one was the real Brent—the guy who goes down on me like Paige Harper is the only thing on the menu, or the guy who plays BINGO at the old-folks' home and lets everyone else win.

"People are complicated, Paige," he'd said with a smile— the one from his campaign ads. "Why can't I be both?"

Because one is a lie, I'd almost said, but rethought it. Granted, I mostly rethought it because at that point in the conversation he'd been ready to prove his allegiance in a very direct way. A delicious shiver runs down my spine as I pull into my driveway...to see Giselle on the porch.

"Are. You. Serious?" I say, turning off the engine. She gets up from the porch swing, gives me a cute little half wave and a hair flip that makes me want to scalp her. As always with Giselle, a bubble of resentment begins in my stomach, floating its way to my mouth. In the past, I've always been quick enough to get away from her before it makes up words of its own and gets out past my lips. Tonight, one of us might not be so lucky.

"Paige," she says as I climb the steps. "Sooo good to see you!"

She always says that, like seeing me is sooo awesome she has to overuse vowels. "Giselle," I say stiffly. "How are you?"

She moves in for her usual air kiss, but I dodge it. "I'm great," she says, letting the rebuff go. "Are you okay?" she asks, eyeing my bandaged arm.

"I'm fine. What do you want?" I ask, my annoyance clear in my voice.

She either doesn't recognize my tone, or is doing everything in her power to ignore it. "I've brought you something!" she says, her voice bubbly and bright.

She whips a bouquet of red roses from behind her back, but I turn away, fiddling with my keys. "Sorry, I'm already spoken for. Maybe you hadn't heard?"

It's a nice little dig. A reminder of her place—and mine.

"Silly!" she squeals, batting my shoulder. "Of course I know that. You two are the perfect couple, the type you can see growing old together, or at least, *I* think you are."

I wince. She got a good one in there. Did Brent tell her about the botched proposal? Did he cry into her glorious red tresses while he told her about finding me in a car with Nico Tralano?

"These are for you," she says, pressing the roses toward me. "From Brent, of course," she clarifies.

"Thanks," I say, and take them from her, tossing then into the front room and pulling the door closed again. "Anything else?" I ask her.

"Yes..." Her eyes cut to the door dubiously, but she's always been good at her job—good at jumping to Brent's every beck and call—so she won't leave until she's done it all, and done it right. "These are also for you," she says quietly, handing me a box of chocolates.

"Great," I say, opening the door again, and tossing the chocolates inside. This time a cry of, *"Candy!"* comes from Shauna before I can pull the door closed.

Giselle cranes her neck, curious—I'm sure—to get a good look at my insane ex-sister-in-law. The one that will wreck my life and Brent's career if we ever do get married.

"Is that all?" I ask, arms crossed.

There's a flicker in Giselle's eyes, one I wouldn't have expected to see. A flash of the temper that lurks underneath that ivory complexion, little roses of heat blooming in her cheeks. She steps toward me, her perfectly outlined upper lip curling back from her pristinely white teeth in a snarl.

"You listen to me, Paige Harper," she says, my name coming out of her mouth like poison, the excited greeting I'd earned by simply arriving at my own home long gone. "That man is going to be somebody someday, and I'm climbing that ladder with him. You can come along for the ride or not, but I won't be treated like this."

"Like what?" I ask. "Like Relationship Repair Delivery Service? Because that's kind of what you are right now, and I'm not the one that asked you to do it."

"No," she says, tossing her hair again. "You don't ask for anything, do you? It all just lands in your lap. That man. This house. Oh, no...wait. This is your ex-husband's house, isn't it? The fae?"

"You're done," I say. "Get off my porch."

"Don't you mean Jax's porch?" she smiles sweetly, backpedaling just far enough out of my reach that I can't take a swipe at her. "Lovely, by the way. Although it's still a little early to start decorating for Halloween, or did something actually die on your doorstep?"

"What?" I've got my hand on the door again, very ready to be done with this night. I turn back around. "What are you talking about?"

But Giselle is already in the driveway, hailing her Uber by flashing her phone. I'm halfway tempted to hop in my car and follow her ride, double-check that she's going home and not straight to Brent to report...or more.

I shake my head. Jax cheating on me has put me on high alert—a place somewhere Brent doesn't deserve to be. I take a deep breath, promise myself I'll text him once I get inside. Get settled. Get calmed down.

Something crunches under my shoe and I step back, perplexed.

Across the entryway, tiny, fragile white bones have been arranged in a message.

STOP.

"Feline bones," Nico says the next morning, flicking the tip of his finger through what's left of the ominous message as he kneels by the front door. He'd just showed up uninvited. And while I don't want to make a habit of this, I can't say I'm angry right now. At least I can confide in him without worrying he'll lose his shit.

"You don't have a cat, do you?" Nico asks, glancing around. "Or rather, you *didn't* have a cat?"

"No," I say, crossing my arms across my chest. But I do hear the lady next door calling for her cat, TomTom Petty, to come home every evening. "Are you sure it's a cat?"

Nico breaks a bone in half and sucks some marrow out. "Yep," he replies, tossing it aside.

"Did you really have to—"

"You asked," Nico says, with a shrug. "It's a cat. Also, it wasn't a shifter. That was straight up *felis catus*."

"Poor TomTom Petty," I say, eyeing the bones. "Wait— shifters can be regular house cats?"

I'd heard of the flashier shifters. Werewolves, of course,

but also all the species of cats. Lions. Panthers. Cheetahs. But a domestic cat?

"Yeah," Nico nods. "You don't hear about them as much because humans don't find them as interesting, or as dangerous. But they're wrong." He taps his eye patch. "I lost my eye to a cat shifter."

"Damn," I say. "Balls to the walls and claws out, huh?"

"No balls," Nico says, shaking his head "It was my mission partner, and kind of my girlfriend...of sorts. And she did this to me."

TomTom Petty no longer has my attention. "Wait, so your housecat ex-girlfriend dug your eye out?"

"Yep," Nico confirms, tossing one last bone aside as he rises.

Wow. That definitely makes me feel less guilty at forgetting to text Brent last night for the flowers and chocolates. I was so freaked out by the bones on my doorstep, I basically just ran inside and flipped the lock behind me. "And I thought my love life was complicated."

"Is it?" Nico asks, cocking his head at me. "Your ex-husband is a fae who is also your landlord, and your current squeeze is a supe-hating politician who accidentally blasted you with a stun gun. Seems pretty straightforward to me."

I raise an eyebrow, searching for a witty retort, but Shauna pulls the front door open. "Did he bring candy, too?" she asks, eyes sweeping Nico. She sniffs. "It smells like blood out here."

"No candy," I say, quickly kicking aside the pile of bones. Shauna and Darron don't know about the eerie message from last night, and I'm going to keep it that way. I need to keep Shauna from getting in my way again. And Darron...well, why freak him out unnecessarily? After my last conversation with Jax, there's no doubt in my mind that

O.H.I.O wants me to stop digging. But if they think knocking off a neighborhood pussycat is going to do it, they've underestimated this girl.

Shauna had already eaten herself into a chocolate coma by the time I made it inside last night, a two-pound box of Godiva digesting in her stomach as she sawed logs on the floor. Judging by the dark smear across her chin, she just now came out of it.

"What'd you get out of Kirkland?" she asks, knuckling one eye.

"Not much, after you punched a hole in him," I tell her. And add, just to beat her to the punch, "You're staying away from him."

"What, it's not take-your-fae-ex-sister-in-law-to-work day?" she asks, batting her eyelashes. Beside me, Nico feigns a cough to cover a laugh. Irritated, I spin on my heel and head for Nico's car, very done with the conversation.

"Oh, but it's take-your-pet-werewolf-dong-along day?" Shauna screeches after us. I get into the passenger seat with cheeks as red as apples. Nico reverses down the drive, giving me a moment of peace to collect myself as we head over to our offices.

My office, I correct myself. My office and his office. Two separate places for two separate and incompatible people. Or one person and one supe, that is.

"I do have transportation of my own," I remind Nico.

He flicks a quick look my way and then shrugs. "Figured it'd be best if we got there at the same time and picking you up seemed easier than synchronizing our watches."

"Okay," I say, but I have a nagging feeling that there's something else Nico isn't telling me. Before I can pursue it, he goes back to asking about my dead kitty bones.

"About that message on your doorstep. Who've you made mad lately?" Nico asks.

"The whole list or you just want a top five?" I ask, grimacing.

"I've got time," Nico says, indicating the red light.

"Well, I completely botched Brent's proposal of marriage, his gorgeous aide-de-camp thinks I don't deserve him, Shauna can kind of go whichever way the wind blows, apparently I got my neighbor's cat killed, and there's the girl at the shooting range who never forgave me for needing extra help from her instructor boyfriend and now sends me shitty Facebook messages whenever she's had too much to drink. Oh, and also a secret underground supe-experimentation group that my ex-husband keeps warning me away from."

"Probably that last one," Nico says, glancing up as the light switches to green.

"Ya think?" I snort back.

"I wouldn't underestimate a jealous girlfriend with a drinking problem, though," he says, and checks the rearview mirror, adding, "We don't seem to have a tail, at least."

My mind is still pondering the fact that shifters can be house cats so it takes me a second to process that Nico is saying we're not being followed. I resist the urge to spin around in my seat, just to be sure.

"You think they might know we have Kirkland?" I ask, as we pull into the parking lot in front of Down & Dirty Supernatural Cleaning Services.

"No," Nico says, snapping off the ignition. "If they knew we had him, that message would've been for me, and written in your bones, not TomTom Petty's."

"Overestimate your worth much?" I ask as I step out of

Nico's car and head for my office door. Before I can get the key in the lock, Nico moves, placing himself in front of my door.

"Hold up, we gotta get on the same page before we go in there," he says.

I frown. "Same page? That right there could've been a perfect Paige pun and you totally missed it." I'm so disappointed by the missed punportunity that it takes me a minute to register what Nico is actually saying. "Also, how are we not on the same page? We need to find out what Kirkland knows? That's one page and I'm the other. And you're not getting on this one." I poke a finger into my own chest. "And that's how you pun," I can't help but add.

I expect a smile or even a groan from Nico, but instead he looks totally serious. Finally, with a sigh, he says, "Paige, I came back here last night and questioned Kirkland by myself."

I step back as if he pushed me. It's not that I'm pissed. Although I am. But that's to be expected. The thing that has me reeling is that familiar old feeling of betrayal. The same one that was like a punch in the gut on that long ago day when I walked in on Jax banging that pixie.

These past few days I've been so focused on fighting my attraction to Nico. But that's just my body talking to his and can be ignored the same way I handle my Twinkie craving at the grocery store. I remind myself they're unnatural and very very bad for me.

Somehow, though, when I wasn't paying attention, while resisting putting my body on Nico's, I failed to stop myself from putting my trust in him. I actually saw us as a team.

And now, I'm hurt. Deeply.

I can't believe I'm such an idiot. I'm almost as disgusted with myself as I am with Nico.

Almost.

"You know that I'm in a time crunch. Not only do you question him without me but you don't let me know immediately what you found out? I have two days. Two. Today and tomorrow. Before my house may belong to some card shark supe," I fume. "You asshole," I say at last, my voice low and angry

"Yeah, I knew you'd say that," he says with a shake of his head. Like I'm the unreasonable one here.

"Because it's true?"

"Because you don't trust me to do my job without looking over my shoulder the whole time!" Nico shoots back.

"Looking over your shoulder?" I echo. And there's the hurt again. He talks like he's been trying to shake me off this whole time.

"All right, just calm down and let me explain," Nico says.

My hands go into fists and I consider taking a swing at him even though it's far more likely to hurt me than him. Telling women to "calm down" must be in chapter one of some secret MANual that all dudes get a copy of at puberty. The chapter is probably entitled: Bitches Be Crazy.

"Explain," I say to Nico, grinding the word out between my teeth.

"Last night after you left, I got to thinking. Fae have powers. They're different. Some manipulate fire. Others water or air or...plants."

"Like Vee," I say, and then I can't help but add, "So, you quickly turned around to tell me this so we could go back and make sure Kirkland was still securely locked up." I open my eyes wide with faux innocence and clap a hand over my mouth. "Oh wait! You didn't do that at all, did you?"

Nico's eyes narrow. "No. We'd had a long day. You looked tired—"

"While you're the big strong werewolf who can go all night," I interject.

He ignores this. "I decided to check on Kirkland and while I was there, maybe see if I could get him to talk. Man to man."

"Or do you mean supe to supe?" I ask sourly.

"Yeah, maybe that too," Nico acknowledges softly.

"And," I add, "you wanted to grill him about your vampire serial killer. Didn't you? That's the only reason you're helping me clear Jax's name. Because there might be something in it for you."

"That's rich coming from you." Nico laughs bitterly. "The only reason you care about freeing your ex-husband, a person who you know is innocent, is because you might lose your house if he stays in jail. Don't lecture me about ulterior motives."

"I was up-front about my motives!" I shoot back, refusing to be shamed. "And I never tried to cut you out, even when it makes me sick working with a supe."

Nico's mouth twists at this and he takes a step closer to me. Putting my chin up, I refuse to budge. "I don't think I make you sick at all, Paige." His hands shoot out, grabbing hold of my hips and suddenly my body is locked against his. "I think the opposite is true and that makes you sick. But you still came knocking at my door, didn't you?"

His right hand runs up my side, sparking shivers everywhere it touches. And then his fingers slide over my face until he grips my chin, forcing my head up so that my eyes meet his lone one. "Admit why you wanted to work with me, Paige."

I stare at him and that one bright blue eye that seems

like it can see all the way through me. I move my neck, sliding out of his grasp, although his hand remains touching my face. I turn so that my lips rub against his thumb. His eye darkens and a low rumble comes from his throat.

"This is why," I say, my voice low and husky.

Then I sink my teeth into his thumb, doing my damnedest to reach bone.

"FUCK!" Nico hollers. He shakes me off, although I hang on like a rabid dog. "You're crazy!" he says as I finally unclench my jaw.

"Yeah," I agree, spitting out his blood on the sidewalk. "Maybe next time you'll think twice before fucking with me."

He says nothing to this, just wraps his bleeding thumb in the tail end of his T-shirt.

I wipe my mouth and then walk to my door, which Nico is no longer blocking. Before I go in, though, I need to know—

"Did he tell you anything?"

"I only got a name out of him, and then..." Nico trails off, rubbing a hand through his hair. "Well, go ahead and look for yourself."

I don't want to look. I want to go home, climb into bed with a bottle of wine, and pull the covers over my head. But I can't do that because I have one day left to free Jax and save my house.

There's also the small matter of my pride. Although that's currently feeling like a very small matter.

Still, I force my head high as I turn the key in the lock and then shove my door open.

Immediately, I'm assaulted by the smell of smoke. Coughing, I spin around to glare at Nico.

He at least has the grace to look chagrined. "I opened

the door last night to air it out, but..." He shrugs as he trails off.

I take a step in further and see a large section of blackened wall near my storage closet. My heart beats faster as I think of Vee. Why I care about that stupid plant, I don't know. But I guess it's hard not to grow attached to something you have to feed daily.

Rushing to the storage room, I throw the door open. The whole room is singed black. There is no sign of Vee. But Kirkland is still there. Or at least I'm pretty sure the charred body on the floor is him.

22

"It turns out our friend Kirkland was not one of the plant-power types of fae," Nico says into the silence.

Furious, I throw myself at him and grab the front of his shirt. "Where is Vee?"

"I didn't see her last night," he swallows. "I assume he ashed her before I got here."

I stumble back, swallowing against tears.

Nico going behind my back. A dead body in my storage closet. And now Vee, dead. It's all too much...

Something tickles the back of my neck. I swat it away, thinking it's a stray hair. But this is too strong for a hair and it curls around my hand. Spinning, I find a vine hanging from the ceiling. I look up to see one of the ceiling tiles missing and Vee up among the wiring hidden behind the panels.

"Vee!" I cry as she drops into my arms. I hug her pot tightly, feeling like an idiot, but not caring.

"Giselle," Nico says when I finally stop stroking Vee's leaves. "That was the name he gave."

Gi-fucking-selle. I try to make my muscles relax but Nico

must see the recognition written on my face. "Mean anything to you?" he asks.

"Nope," I answer quickly.

Nico's eyes narrow. "How come you're pursing your lips, then? You do that when you're thinking."

I force my lips into a smile. "I was thinking, actually." I hold out a hand. "Give me your car keys. I'm taking Vee home so she can get some clean air."

"I'll drive you."

"The hell you will," I snap. "You can stay here and do your best to restore my office before I see it again. Get the smoke out. Remove the dead body. I'm assuming you know how to do that." He gives me a tight nod and I continue, "Also sweep up the ashes. Being a big strong supe, I'm sure you can handle a little cleaning. But just in case it's been a while since you've handled a sponge, here's a little tip— don't be afraid to get dirty. Although I doubt that will be a problem for you."

With that, Vee and I exit, the bell on my door tinkling merrily behind us.

Vee actually snuggles with me as we drive back to the house, rubbing her lower jaw against my shoulder while her pot teeters precariously on the passenger seat. Darron looks dubious when I float into the front hall with her nestled in my elbow, but Shauna takes her from me carefully, holding her like a baby.

"That's a good girl," Shauna coos. "I'm going to get you set up somewhere nice, with lots of sunlight and fresh air. And I'll open the window, too. There's plenty of cats in the neighborhood—"

"No eating cats," I yell over my shoulder as I head up to my attic bedroom, shuddering as I think of poor TomTom-Petty. "Keep that window closed!"

I throw myself across my bed, pondering my next move.

Giselle...God, it makes my blood boil to think about her sitting on my porch swing, probably wiping blood off her hands after dismembering poor TomTomPetty.

And she's not the only one on my shit list. Nico had the balls to go into my own office without me, and question Kirkland behind my back. Whatever Nico's methods were, I'm sure it wasn't pretty. But I deserved a shot at Kirkland. Maybe plain old persuasion could have gotten more than a single name out of him.

Because even if Giselle is Kirkland's contact within O.H.I.O, she's definitely just a foot soldier. I have no doubt she could sleep her way to the top, but somebody with rank doesn't get sent to deliver messages spelled in cat bones. And I'm confident that Giselle isn't intimidating enough to make Kirkland ignite his own power, burning himself alive before he gave up more names. Names of the people at the top, people that he was either so loyal to he'd die to protect them, or he knew they'd do something much worse to him than burn him alive if he walked away from an interrogation.

Either way, it puts me in a tough spot.

Whoever is at the top of that food chain wants Jax framed for murder, and for me to stop sticking my nose where it doesn't belong. Flicking through my phone, I find my last text conversation with Brent. Maybe I'll throw them for a loop by sticking my nose somewhere it's been plenty of times—and I've never had any complaints.

Typically, getting Brent to walk away from work is diffi-cult. But we found out early on in our relationship that we're both really good at the same thing—going down. So I send him the blowjob emoji—the surprised "O" face—and get a response immediately.

I'll be right over.

I'm sure he thinks I'm about to apologize for all my bad behavior lately. Screwing up what should have been a perfect proposal, hanging out with Nico Tralano, throwing his candy and flowers around, and kicking Giselle off my front porch.

I'm not going to apologize for shit, but I don't exactly think a text "fingering" his right-hand-woman as part of a supe-experimentation ring would get him over here as quickly as the possibility of a blowjob.

I wait for him out on the porch, busying myself with a broom while I wait. There's barely time to sweep away the last bits of Tom Tom Petty before brakes squeal on the front drive. Leaving the broom behind, I head down the steps to greet Brent on the front walk.

"Hey babe," he says. He's got his naughty smile on, not his kissing babies one. He's dressed for campaigning, looking sharp in a three-piece suit. I almost consider making good on my emoji promise, but decide it's best to take care of business first. I can go down later on; right now I need to get the dirty part out of the way.

I take Brent by the hand and lead him to the porch swing. "We need to talk," I say.

"Oh, I thought..." The smile fades, replaced by mild confusion.

"Listen," I say, twining my fingers with his. "I know things have been difficult between us lately. But I need you to hear me out about something."

"Paige, of course," he says, covering both our hands with his other one. "What's going on? You look upset."

"You've got a snake in the grass in your campaign," I say.

"What?" Brent's eyebrows fly up, and he lets go of my hands, both of his becoming fists. "Who is it? What do they know and who have they told?"

I hope that anger holds on as I take the plunge. "It's Giselle."

23

"Not possible." Brent shakes his head, his rage disappearing. "You've never liked her, I know, but you have to understand—"

"You're the one that has to understand!" I yell, my chill disappearing. It's not that I thought Brent would immediately hop on board the 'Giselle is bad' train, but damn, he didn't even consider it for two seconds. And then to twist things so that it's about me not liking her. That fires me right up.

Getting up from the swing, I pace the length of the porch. "Look, I've been working on clearing Jax's name. Not because I still love him, but because he put my house on the line in some big supe poker game. If he loses my house..."

I stare at Brent, begging him to understand. And for the first time, he kinda does.

"You love this house," he says, softly. "I know. Sometimes I think that I'm more jealous of this house than I am of Jax." He takes a deep breath and then lets it out slowly. "But then I remind myself that it has all these memories of better times with your parents."

Tears fill my eyes. "Yes! Exactly! I know you think I need to move on, but not like this. Not having it stolen away from me." I scrub away the tears with the back of my fist. "I thought if I can give the police the actual killer, then Jax will go free. That's why I was with Nico. He's been helping me—"

"Out of the goodness of his heart," Brent interrupts dryly.

"Ha. No. Definitely not. I'm not even sure he has a heart," I sneer. "We just happened to have similar goals for a short time." I frown. "Until we didn't." The anger at Nico wells up all over again. When I saw him on my porch this morning I actually thought it was a sweet gesture. Not that he was trying to head me off at the pass. I am such an idiot sometimes.

"Paige?" Brent's hand closes around mine, brings me back to the present.

"Right, so anyway, we found this fae guy who set up the cleaning job that got me to ..."

"Witness Jax standing over the murder victim with a knife in his hand?" Brent helpfully fills in. "Or do you prefer 'where you fingered him'?"

I give him a sour look. "Anyway, Nico tried to persuade the faerie to give up what he knew. Turns out strong-arming him wasn't the right tactic, because the dude self-immolated."

Brent's eyebrows rise. "Wow."

"Yeah."

"But then how does poor innocent Giselle tie into this?" Brent asks gently, humoring me.

"Poor innocent Giselle my ass!" I say, emphasizing it with a slap to my own hind quarters. "The fae said her name. That's the one bit of info he dropped. Which means that she's part of an anti-supe organization. A fringe group that even Humans First might have issues with. They recruit supes for experiments, drawing them in with all kinds of promises, but then—"

"Wait, wait, wait..." Brent says. "You're raving."

"I'm not *raving*," I shout, stomping my foot. "And I'm not making this up and it's not jealousy. If she's exposed it will not look good for you, Brent! This organization—"

"Let's start there," Brent says smoothly, his calm debate tone kicking in. "If you want me to hear you out, you need to start talking sense. What is this organization called?"

I press my lips together, aware that the answer won't win me points. "O.H.I.O."

"Like the state?" Brent asks, and God bless him, he's not laughing.

"Yes," I say, relieved. "It stands for Order for Human Improvement Options."

Brent pulls his phone out of his pocket and begins tapping away with his thumbs.

"You won't find it online," I tell him. "It's very underground. Very dangerous."

"And how did you find out about them?"

I take a deep breath, exhale slowly. "Jax was involved with them. They're trying to frame him for the vampire murders, because he threatened to talk, to expose people if he didn't get what he wanted."

"Oh, so your ex-husband is the one who told you that my aide who you've always hated is involved in supe-trafficking?" Brent shakes his head. "I think I see what's going on."

"Brent, I'm serious!" I follow him to the porch steps, grabbing his arm. "She...she...she killed TomTom Petty!"

"She killed who?"

"TomTom Petty," I say, wiping tears of frustration out of my eyes. "The neighbor's cat." I know I sound ridiculous and I can tell from the look on his face that I'm losing him.

"Maybe you need a break," he tells me. "From work, from this." He motions to the house. "Why don't you come and stay with me for a while? Let other people clean up their own messes for once." He takes my hand, pulls me back to sitting.

"I know that you've been burned in the marriage department. I should have thought of that before I proposed. If you don't want to get married right away, that's fine. Let's just live in sin for a bit."

"That won't play well with your older voters..." I start.

"Well, too bad!" He grins. "A vote for me is a vote for you, and I want you by my side."

I'm touched. Brent is willing to sacrifice votes for me. It means he really cares.

"Maybe that's not such a bad idea..." I start. "But I really think Jax is innocent..."

"I'll pull some strings." He rubs my hand. "Let me look into it. Get him a top-notch lawyer. If he's not guilty I'll make sure he gets out. Then he can also be out of your life for good."

"That sounds really great, actually." I want to be done with this part of my life. I want to move on. But I'm still clinging to the past. To my parents who have been gone for two years. To this house. To my business.

"Then you won't have to deal with supes anymore. No werewolf PIs. No pixie in-laws. No random fae clients getting themselves killed."

I nod. Why not? Why not just let Brent take care of it—

take care of me? I lean into him and he puts his arm around me.

"What about Giselle?" I ask.

"I'll look into that too. I promise if there's any proof that she's trying to sabotage my campaign, she'll be gone so fast your head will spin. Although I honestly cannot see her being a criminal mastermind. Do you think that maybe there could possibly be two Giselles in the world?"

Shit. He's right. "I guess…"

"And if Kirkland was under duress, well, studies have shown that those types of confessions usually don't hold up."

My whole body stiffens in Brent's arms. I run back through everything I told him. I'm pretty certain I didn't say Kirkland's name. Honestly, after seeing his charred remains, I never want to even think his name again.

"Paige, what's wrong?" Brent asks, rubbing his hand on my back.

I look up at him. He looks back at me, solid and steady. Making me doubt myself. I mean, this is Brent. My straight as an arrow guy. My safe choice.

"I never told you Kirkland's name," I say in a low voice.

He chuckles indulgently. "Sweetie, I know you have trust issues after everything with Jax. But this is taking things a little too far, isn't it?"

I stare, wondering if I'm going crazy. I never said Kirkland's name. The more I think about it, the more certain I am.

Is Brent fucking gaslighting me?

"I never said his name," I say again, this time louder.

His handsome features cloud. "Sure you did, baby."

"Don't call me baby. I'm not a sweet naive young thing.

Like Giselle." Stars explode behind my eyes as pieces start to connect. "She would do anything for you. She would murder someone for you."

I pull away from Brent but he holds me firm. "I do love how clever you are. But it makes you such a pain in my ass sometimes."

This is that side of Brent that I rarely get to see. The cruel one. "I'm a pain...?"

"Yes, Paige. You pain me. I love you with everything I have. I was willing to overlook your quirks, your past relationships, your living situation, because I want to be with you."

"You want to mold me into a perfect little wife. You want me to be someone else!" I shout.

"No! I want you to be you, but better. A woman fit for a Senator, for the President.

"And O.H.I.O will help get you there," I say quietly. He's been a part of it from the beginning.

"You knew my ambitions when you met me," he says, as if that explains it all.

"Why? Why the murder? Why the frame up?"

"I wanted Jax out of the way. Kit was a convenient pawn. He was on our payroll and related to Jax. It fell in my lap!"

"But why involve me..." Even as I ask, the answer occurs to me. "You wanted me to be the one to discover Jax, because you wanted me to literally see him with blood on his hands. It wasn't enough for you to lock him up, you wanted to make me hate him."

"Again, you are a clever girl," he tells me, like somehow he's trying to congratulate me.

"I wish I was clever enough to never have gotten involved with you," I snap, trying to jerk away once more. Brent just grips me tighter.

"You ungrateful little bitch," he hisses. "Do you know how much I have done for you? Giselle said you're not worth it, but I defended you. I told her that I love you. That you are the only woman for me." Jerking me into him so that my boobs mash against his chest, he lowers his face to mine.

I bare my teeth just before his mouth covers mine. Realizing he's not going to take no for an answer, I open my mouth, allowing his tongue inside.

"That's right, baby," he says. "Open up for me."

I bite down. Hard.

"AAAUUUGHH!" Brent flings me to the porch floor. I hit the wood hard and when I try to catch myself a jolt of pain shoots up my arm.

"You bitch!" Brent hollers, blood pouring from his mouth. I manage to roll away as he kicks at me and catches the tip of his shoe in my left kidney. It hurts like a bitch.

I'm not out of danger yet, though. Brent advances on me with murder in his eyes as I desperately scramble to my feet.

"I did it all for you," he says, his words distorted. He spits out a mouthful of blood.

I can't believe any of this. "Brent, despite whatever those O.H.I.O people told you, you'll never get away with this."

He laughs at this and the sound is a little maniacal. The blood still pouring from his mouth and dripping down his chin doesn't help. "You are just a little cleaning lady, too smart for your own good." Emphasizing this last word, he reaches out and snatches me. His fingers press into my upper arms in a way that promises to leave bruises tomorrow.

"Stop! Brent!" I try to get him to look into my eyes. To see me. But it's like he's been lost to a darker place. "Please, you're hurting me!"

"If I can't have you, no one can!" He pushes me back

until I slam against the front window. One of his hands releases my arm only to slide across my breast and then up to my throat. He stops there and using the tips of his fingers, strokes the soft skin there. "I love you," he says softly.

And then he starts to squeeze.

24

———

Female Who Fingered Fae Finished by Fiancé.

That's what the headlines will read.

I grab hold of Brent's hand that's cutting off my air supply and pull with all my might. He barely budges.

"I've killed men this way before," he says to me almost conversationally. "But never a woman."

"You killed...k...k...k...?" I gasp.

"Yes. I killed Kit," he says with finality.

"Hey honey," comes a sassy voice from behind Brent. "I hope you don't mind that you're on camera." Releasing me, Brent whirls around to find a smiling Daphne, dressed in a pair of Rita Heyworth short shorts and a crop top, standing in the doorway. She waggles her fingers at the two of us. "I've been watching your convo, and I have to say it's pretty juicy stuff. You're basically the poster boy for toxic masculinity. So, should I call the cops first, or the news outlets?"

"What camera?" Brent demands.

"Door cam," Daphne answers. She jerks her head to the left where I notice a newly installed doorbell. "Paige tried to keep the weird animal sacrifice a secret, but my mama didn't raise a fool. What kind of man did your mama raise?"

Brent takes a threatening step toward Daphne. "Give me your phone. Now," he demands. "You perverted little fruitcake..."

"Fuck you, Brent," I say, my voice raspy. Reaching behind me, my fingers close around the broom I left leaning against the wall. Gripping it like a baseball bat, I aim for Brent's big fat head—and swing.

It makes contact, he trips and bashes his head on one of my flowerpots, shattering it and knocking him out cold. He lies there like a sack of bricks.

Daphne puts her hands on her immaculately padded hips. "What now?"

"Make me a copy of that video. I'm calling the cops."

———

Detective McGinnis isn't available but his partner, Detective Sloane, shows up and takes Brent away in handcuffs. He takes a copy of the video too, gets all the info on what's been going on for the last few days. I tell him everything. Well, almost. I conveniently leave out the part about the dead fae in my office. I have to say, it's immensely satisfying to see Brent placed into the back of a squad car.

Actually, it's satisfying to see the asshole who just assaulted me on my own porch led away in handcuffs. But my brain still hasn't totally accepted that this guy is Brent. My Brent.

I've been beating myself up for not being ready to commit to him. I was so certain that he was a good guy. The type that you spend the rest of your life regretting letting get away. And now there Brent goes as the cop car pulls away from the curb.

How bad is my judgment? And my taste in men?

I justified my marriage to Jax by saying I was young and didn't know better.

But I'm supposed to be older and wiser.

Why do I keep putting my trust in the wrong people? Jax. Nico. Brent.

Suddenly, I'm hit with a wave of longing so intense it nearly knocks me down. I want my dad. I want my mom. They were my soft place to fall. I always knew that no matter what happened they would be there for me. Now with them gone, I am all alone. Mostly, I try not to think about it, but at times like this the loss feels fresh again.

I'm not the only one who's upset.

When Shauna finds out she not only missed all the excitement, but missed her chance to kill Kit's murderer...well, to say she loses her shit is an understatement. The kitchen is wrecked. Shauna smashed all the dishes she was meant to wash yesterday. Then she started throwing around the pots and pans.

"I'd stay with her," I tell Daphne, even though in all honesty I'd rather go up to the attic and lick my wounds in private. "But I've got to head to the office and make sure some things have been...cleaned." It will look terrible if the cops find a burnt body in my storage closet. I don't know what tale Brent is going to spin, but I need to look squeaky clean.

"I'll keep Shauna busy today," he assures me as something shatters in the background. "Maybe go to a spa, let her get some beauty in her." I know her casual drug use can be a slippery slope, but I honestly do not have a better idea.

"Thank you." I tell her. "Shauna really responds to you.

And thank you for distracting Brent and basically saving my life."

Daphne grins. "A fairy drag mother's work is never done. But you are very welcome." She pauses. "At least this means Jax will get out in time for his game tomorrow."

"Silver lining," I agree. Why is my only hope Jax playing a game of poker to not lose the house that he shouldn't have put up as collateral to begin with?

I head to my office, putting the chaos of my house in my rearview mirror. But I get the distinct feeling that I'm jumping out of the frying pan into the fire. I push open my office door, dreading what I will find. But everything looks fairly decent. I mean, it smells a bit smoky but there's no dead body in the closet, so that's a big win. If Brent tells the cops about the dead fae, I can always say there was a fire and Brent must be twisting that to screw me over.

I fumble with my keys at the office door. I've almost got it when I hear Nico pull into the parking spot directly behind me, so close I can feel the heat from his car on the back of my legs, as warm as his breath on my neck inside that stupid, small closet.

"Hey Paige," he says. I can't ignore him, so I turn around, which gives him a good look at the bruises on my neck. The marks from Brent's fingers have purpled in a way that no amount of makeup can fully cover up.

A muscle in his jaw flickers, a flare lighting in his eye. "What happened to you?"

"Nothing. It's none of your business," I tell him, swinging open my office door.

"Well, I cleaned up that...mess..." he starts.

"You mean the mess that you created?" I spit out. "Congratulations, do you want a parade?"

"I guess you're still angry."

"Of course I'm still angry, you jerk!" I fume. How could I not be? He treated me like a helpless human. And I was almost murdered this morning. Not that he knows that, although he did just ask and I told him it wasn't his business.

Nico takes a step back, his expression hardening, confusion on his face. "So this is how it's going to be, huh? Back to your frosty bitch act every time we run into each other?"

"I don't have time for this," I tell him. "You were actually zero help on the case. I don't need you. You're fired. Don't expect to get paid."

"You weren't paying me to begin with!" he yells.

"Lose my number, too!" I yell back as I slam the office door behind me. I'm done with Nico Tralano. He's proved himself to be as unreliable as any other supe. From now on. I'll ignore his presence. I'll ignore the screams of ecstasy from his clients. I'll invest in a good set of ear plugs. All curiosity about his package will cease.

I sit down at my desk and notice I have a voicemail.

"Hi, Paige, this is Liam. You know...from the straw party? I saved you from the blinged out vamp. Well, I didn't actually save you. You still got cut, I guess. So...I guess I just wanted to say hi and that it was nice to meet you the other day and, wow I am terrible at leaving messages. This isn't a social call, I promise, unless you want it to be. I might have a cleaning gig for you. Let me know if you're interested."

Despite everything I can't help but smile at Liam's adorkable message. I will definitely call him back, I need the money, but I also need normal people in my life. My heart sinks. If he *is* normal. I mean, how can you even tell anymore? I will definitely not be getting romantically involved with him. I am done with dating for a good long while.

I boot up my computer and my smile fades when I read the news. There's nothing about Brent. About O.H.I.O. About the whole conspiracy. I click through until I'm sure I'm not missing something, then I call the number for McGinnis.

He picks up and I start to ask if the media is waiting to break the story or what, but he hushes me.

"Listen, I can't talk about this right now." His voice is low and heavy, clearly worried about someone listening in. "Can I drop by later?"

"Yes," I tell him, my mistrust heavy in my tone. "But it will *not* be a short conversation. I want answers."

"I hear you," McGinnis assures me.

Speaking of hearing things, Miss Red Ferrari pulls in just as I'm hanging up, which means I'm about to be hearing a whole hell of a lot of things I don't want to.

I'm digging around in the back room for something I can stick in my ears—plugs, paper towels, little burnt pieces of fae—when I hear my office door bang open.

"Paige?!?!" a voice cries out, and my heart leaps into my throat. I'd know that scream of deep neediness anywhere.

"Jax!?" I pop out of the backroom to find my ex-husband leaning against my desk, not in a sauve-supe way, but in a catch-my-breath kind of way. His knuckles are bandaged and one of his eyes is black.

"What happened?" I ask, going to him.

"It doesn't matter." Jax waves my confusion off. "I need to get to the poker game—now. I flew this far but..." He takes a deep breath, his exhaustion obvious.

"But the game isn't until tomorrow," I tell him. "You said it was this weekend." I point at my day-by-day calendar, and the large black *Friday* printed at the top.

"Friday *is* the weekend, Paige!" Jax practically yells.

"It's really not," I argue. "Friday is part of the work week—"

"We can fight about a calendar that's been in use since the fifteenth century, or you can get your priorities in order. The game starts in twenty minutes."

"Twenty minutes!" I screech. "Where's it even at?"

He gives me an address that's easily half an hour across town, and that's if I hit lights right—and zero people.

"Move!" I scream at him, now the panicked one. Jax picks up on my urgency and jogs to Vanna. I'm in the driver's seat when he taps on the window, beckoning me to unlock his door.

"It's not locked," I call, but he shakes his head and jerks the handle. Nothing happens except a blast of hot air from the vents hits me in the face. Oh, shit.

I rest my forehead on the steering wheel. "Vanna," I ask quietly. "Do you not like Jax?"

I get a single, affirmative toot in response. I tighten my finger on the steering wheel. "Look, I understand. I'm not his biggest fan either, but it's really important to me that we get him somewhere. Can you make an exception for me? Just this one time?"

Vanna's answer is for the engine to die. I slap the steering wheel. "You little bi—" I bite the last word off, aware that if she chose to, Vanna could accelerate right into my office window.

I get out, fuming.

"What are we going to do?" Jax asks.

My eye lands on the little red Ferrari.

"Something illegal," I say.

25

I've been driving this Ferrari for approximately two minutes, and I have no idea why its owner also thinks she needs Nico for stimulation. Holy shit, this thing can go. I'm tearing through lights and zipping past people in sedans like they're on bicycles. Jax is next to me, white-knuckling the dashboard.

"Paige, I know I came to you for help, but—"

"Shut up, I really need to concentrate right now," I say, accelerating when I see that I can probably catch the yellow light. I don't, but I'm sure the traffic cam got a good shot of the license plate, and that Nico's client will likely be getting a ticket in the mail soon.

It's hilarious. It's exhilarating. I'm a pretty girl in a fast car, and damn, if I don't like the way this beauty hums under my ass.

Oh and look, there's a seat warmer, too.

"I learned a little bit about O.H.I.O," I tell Jax.

"Don't even say their name," he tells me. "I shouldn't have gotten involved with them to begin with." He touches his black eye.

"Is that who messed you up?" I ask. "Did O.H.I.O get to you in prison?"

"They did. I didn't think I was ever getting out, but low and behold, I get released so fast it makes my head spin."

"That was me," I tell him. "I found out who really killed Kit. It was..." I pause. "It was Brent."

"BRENT?!" Jax whoops. "Are you shitting me? Mr. Perfect Politician. The guy who was supposed to replace me? I knew he was so boring he had to be really terrible."

"Don't be so gleeful, he almost killed me too," I tell him.

"Well, for that I'm going to make sure he gets beaten up in prison. I have some sway with the Devil Wings now. I'll make sure he gets his ass kicked daily."

"Just don't," I tell him. "No more messing with O.H.I.O. Brent is on tape attacking me. He's going down.

"PAIGE!" Jax yells as I nearly side-swipe someone. There's no impact, but there are definitely two birds being flipped at me in the rearview mirror. They recede too quickly for me to care as the speedometer passes 85...and keeps going.

"It's a RESIDENTIAL AREA!" Jax yells as I turn off the freeway. "For the love of—"

He uses some minor god I don't know. Once Jax found out he was a fae he took an online course about mythology. It was the one time he used the computer for something non-pornographic. My phone rings in the cupholder, and I glance down to see it's Nico.

I punch the speaker button. "What?" I demand.

"Did you steal my client's car?" Nico demands. "The guy across the street—"

"The dry cleaner owner?" I ask.

"Nah, that kid who works at the deli," Nico says.

"That little asshole," I say. "He hates me because I always ask to use their bathroom."

"Are you saying he's lying?" Nico asks, his voice dripping with skepticism.

"Oh no, I took the car. I gotta be somewhere--fast. If you throw me under the bus, I'll turn you in for offing Kirkland. I got a buddy on the force now, so I can make it happen real easy."

Nico is silent for so long I'm almost certain he's hung up. But then finally he says, "Paige Harper, I'll cover for you this time. But this is the last time you hold Kirkland over my head. Got it?"

I want to push back, but I don't care enough. "Yeah, fine, whatever," I say and then stab the end button on my phone.

"You're a real ball buster sometimes," Jax says to me.

"Shut up and tell me the house number," I answer, finally slowing down a little when I see a sign—SLOW! Baby Hydra At Play! Of course this game is going down in some dark basement on the supe side of town. Somewhere human cops could care less.

"If I shut up then I can't..." He pauses when he sees my face and tells me the number. I spin into the drive, ignoring the alarmed harpy faces at the window when the curtains pull back. I glance at my watch. "Five minutes to spare."

I expect Jax to jump out and get right to the game. Instead, he grabs me, pulls me close and gives me a kiss that takes me back. Back to before Brent and these bruises on my neck. Back to a time when I still trusted him...even if that was a mistake.

Finally, he pulls away. "You're amazing, Paige, even if you *are* a certified ball buster."

"I know," I tell him. "Now go get my house back."

You'd think nearly being strangled on my front porch would put me off my house, but I still love pulling up in the driveway. Vanna had been more than happy to open her doors and start for me once I made it back to the office. Nico and his client gave me dark looks when I got out of the Ferrari, but all I did was toss her keys to her.

Surprisingly agile, she'd swiped them from the air, her mouth turning into a frown when I said, "Honey, you don't need him when you've got that."

With my adrenaline burning out, I'm forced to recognize the idea that I might lose this house. But I can't. I just can't. It makes me feel safe. It makes me feel home.

My house has never betrayed me.

Darron and Shauna are gone and I notice the doorbell cam is missing too. Did Sloane take it? For evidence maybe? I shudder at the idea of anyone watching Brent strangle me, throw me down, take kicks at me while I curl into a ball.

My phone goes off with a text from Jax.

Hey! This is Canwella, I work the door here for the players. They can't have phones at the table but your man asked that I keep you updated.

I roll my eyes, half-annoyed. I'm imagining Canwella as a gorgeous, fine-boned fae, typing her own number into Jax's phone the second he handed it to her. Another text comes through.

First update: Your man is fine.

On the other hand, maybe this is actually just Jax texting me. Another message comes in, this one from McGinnis.

There in two.

I go to the front door to wait for him on the porch,

glancing down when my phone vibrates with another message from Canwella.

Nice. Got a full house on the river.

I shoot out a response.

No, just a Cape Cod in a good neighborhood.

There's a pause, the ellipsis bubble appears, then disappears, then comes back again. Finally, Canwella responds.

You don't know much about poker, do you?

McGinnis arrives and I usher him into the kitchen, which is absolutely destroyed, remnants of Shauna's temper tantrum covering the floor. I clear off a bit of the table and find a couple of mugs that haven't been smashed.

"Are the police waiting to release the news?" I ask, pouring us coffee. "I know Brent can pull strings, but I'd say I have pretty hard evidence."

Instead of answering my question he points to my neck and whistles. "Brent did that?" I nod. "And that?" he asks about my bandaged arm.

"That was at the straw party when I was trying to find out info. Some greasy vamp with a blinged out straw had a fuzzy concept of consent."

"You really do find trouble," he tells me fondly and for a moment it's like my father is back. I swallow hard, trying to fight my frustrated tears.

"When will Brent be charged?" I ask.

"Paige, he won't be."

I let his words wash over me. "That's impossible. Sloane put him in handcuffs...he took the video..."

"There's no video either," McGinnis cuts in.

I grab my phone to login into the home security site with Darron's password, but the file has been deleted. I slam it down on the counter.

"What's going on?" We caught the bad guy. We did it. That should be the end.

"Your boyfriend must have some very powerful friends," McGinnis says. "Earlier today a man confessed to Kit's murder. Actually, *all* the recent vamp murders."

"I know," I tell him. "I talked to Jax, but he didn't exactly have all the details." Also, I stole a car immediately after that and violated probably twenty traffic laws, but I decide not to mention that.

"Some guy with a record. I did a little quick digging. Apparently, he's got a new baby in the NICU. My bet is he got a lot of money to secure his kid's future while he goes away to prison."

I collapse back into my chair. "Why bother? If Brent isn't going to get charged, why bother getting Jax out?"

"If I were a betting man, I'd wager that your ex wants you to drop it. If you have no skin in the game, you're more likely to do that. Has he been in contact?"

I shake my head. "No. But we're just going to let him get away with it?" I ask. "You're a cop, for fuck's sake."

He grimaces. "I'm a cop who likes being a cop. Sloane too. I don't know what they have on him but for him to do this..." He slams a fist on the table. "What can I do? Fight the whole system? Get myself killed?"

"I don't know." I tell him, deflated.

"Look." He stands. "I want to be a good cop. I'll keep my eyes and ears open. We'll get these bastards, one day. Until then, just lay low."

"I'll try," I tell him.

"Take care of yourself, Paige," McGinnis says before he leaves.

"I always do," I tell him.

After he leaves, another text from Canwella comes through.

Took a beating that hand. Bleak outlook. He's still hot, though. I'd bang him.

There's a pause, then another message comes in.

Kinda stupid though, am I right?

So. Stupid. I text back.

But I can't get over those shoulder blades. Damn.

Finally. Someone who speaks my language.

Canwella, I think you and I are going to be friends.

———

I wake to the sound of the Widow's Walk hatch screeching open. I grab my gun from under my pillow. If that's Brent I won't hesitate to blow his damn head off.

But it's Jax who makes his way down the winding steps, a big smile on his face, even though he looks exhausted. I glance at the clock. It's four in the morning, and that smile can only mean one thing.

I hug a pillow to my chest. "You...you won?!" I ask, barely letting myself hope.

"Of course, I did!" His face is a mixture of pride and arrogance. "Canwella said you guys got to chatting, but you must have fallen asleep because you stopped answering. I came over right away...I mean...I still worry about you, Paige."

"But...you promised never to come into the house again," I say. "We made a fae bargain."

"I said I would never *darken your* doorstep *again*. And I didn't. I used the Widow's Walk."

Sneaky fae bastard. I should have been more specific, should have made him say words that had no wiggle room.

"I hate you so much," I tell him, even though I'm smiling. "And handing over the deed to the house?"

He gives me a piece of paper. "Handed over. I didn't change anything, but now you have a copy of the deed with my name on it...."

I level the gun at him. "Get out."

His smile vanishes. "What did I miss?"

"You're going to be missing a body part if you don't get the hell out of my house."

"Okay, okay." He backs up the spiral staircase. "I'll give you some time to cool off."

"JUST GO!" I shout, throwing a pillow after him as he disappears up the hatch. First thing tomorrow I'm getting a bolt to keep that thing locked.

"Everything okay up there?" Darron yells from the bottom of the attic stairs. I roll out of bed.

"Yeah, fine." I roll my eyes. "Jax won the house back, so we're not homeless."

"Oh, that's great news. But...well, I could actually use some help down here." His voice is a little panicked.

I trudge down the stairs. "Shauna?" I ask.

"No, she's sleeping off her beauty fix." His eyes are wide. "Did you notice the doorbell cam disappeared?"

"I did. I thought the cops took it—"

"Maybe, but it's gone...and it really would have come in handy right about now." He leads me to the front door and throws it open.

On the porch is a dead body. A dead vamp body. It's the jerk from the straw party who stole a taste of my blood. And his black blinged-out straw is sticking out of his neck, impaling a piece of paper onto his throat.

I crouch by him. The note reads, *Clean this up, bitch.*

"Are murders going to be a normal thing around here?" Darron asks.

"I hope not," I tell him as I pull out my phone. But who should I call? All the cops are dirty or scared. I don't have anyone.

I sigh and dial the number. I'm about to eat some major humble pie. I'm never going to hear the end of this from him.

"Hi Nico. I need your help..."

God save me from vampires and werewolves.

THE END

———

Continue the series with the next book **Grime & Punishment, Down & Dirty Book 2!**

Keep reading for a sneak peek at the first chapter of Grime & Punishment, as well as sneak peeks at our other series!

Sign up for our newsletter to receive FREE short stories! Visit www.marleylynn.com/newsletter

Like us on Facebook for books deals, surprise sales, and promotions!
www.facebook.com/MarleyLynnAuthor

SNEAK PEEK: GRIME & PUNISHMENT (DOWN & DIRTY SUPERNATURAL CLEANING SERVICES #2)

1

On the porch of my beautiful Victorian house is a dead body.

A dead *vamp* body. A pool of blood surrounds him, no doubt permanently staining the wooden floorboards. I'll have to get some hydrogen peroxide on that ASAP.

Even worse, it's a vampire I know. I met him at a vampire straw party where I was trying to get information about a *different* dead vampire. This vamp at the party was blinged out in diamonds and used a bedazzled straw to steal a taste of my blood.

If this was a romantic comedy, that would be our meet-cute. A love/hate thing, where he comes on too strong at first, but eventually I come to see the big softie he is inside.

Except my life is definitely not a romantic comedy. Also, that guy was a total asshole through and through. It was real obvious in the three minutes we spent getting to know one another. Still, I didn't want him dead. Or, er, *more* dead since vamps are technically already dead. But this dude in front me of me is a total goner will-bite-no-more dead.

And his black bejeweled straw is sticking out of his neck, impaling a piece of paper onto his throat.

I crouch by him. The note reads, *Clean this up, bitch.*

"Are murders going to be a normal thing around here?" Darron asks. Darron is my housemate, an older thespian and a drag queen. He's lived with me for about a week, but honestly it feels like he moved in a lifetime ago, so much has happened.

"I hope not," I tell him as I pull out my phone. But who should I call? All the cops are dirty or scared. I learned that the hard way this week. I don't have anyone.

Sighing, I scroll through my contacts. I'm about to eat some major humble pie. I'm never going to hear the end of this from him.

"Hi Nico. I need your help..." I practice out loud while the phone rings on the other end. And almost choke on the words.

"Nico?" Darron mouths. "The sexy one-eyed werewolf PI?"

I nod while waiting for Nico to pick up. If he does. Our last interaction did not go well. I basically told him that I never wanted to see him again. He'd lied to me, and I was beyond pissed. Then I stole one of this client's cars—a cute red Ferrari. But that was yesterday, so totally water under the bridge, right?

"What do you want, Paige?" he answers with a growl.

Okay, so maybe more like water washing away the bridge.

"Look, I'm not really sorry about yesterday..."

"You're specifically calling me to *not* apologize?" he asks.

"No. Yes. Just, can you come over?"

"I don't know. I'm busy. I do have clients," he says. I don't know if he means it as a low blow, because my cleaning business has dried up, but it stings. On the other hand, half of his clients are only there for sex-on-the-side so I wouldn't necessarily put all his success on his investigative skills.

"Fine. I'll call someone else about the dead vamp on my porch," I tell him.

"Wait. No. Are you okay?" he asks, his tone morphing from annoyed to fierce.

"I'm great. Except for the previously aforementioned dead vampire on my porch," I snark. "Are you coming or not?"

He pauses long enough to make me think he's gonna say no. But then... "Be there in twenty," he says.

"What do we do with this in the meantime?" Darron motions to the corpse.

I have never been so glad to have a large house away from the street. You'd have to actually walk up to my door to see Dead Mr. Bling Vamp.

I shrug. "Coffee?"

We head toward the kitchen, still trashed from my other housemate's extreme reaction to the bad news that her brother's killer was actually my boyfriend, Brent. And she wasn't there to watch him get arrested. And then tear him into a million tiny pieces. Shauna had a bit of a pixie breakdown, which involves actually breaking things. Mostly my things, but I didn't have the heart to light into her at the time.

I sigh and sit. "Darron, you make the coffee and I'll fill you in."

"Deal," he says and gets started, cleaning as he goes, moving with a grace that I envy. He's really not the worst housemate a girl could have.

"Brent..." I start. How do I even begin?

"Yes, your murderous boyfriend who tried to frame your

ex-husband, Jax, for the murder of the child he was switched with at birth, called a changeling by the fae." He pauses, tilts his head.

"That's the one," I tell him with a sigh.

"Your life is better than a telenovela!" he exclaims.

"Just try living the drama," I mutter before I continue. "Brent's part of this organization. They're pretty powerful actually. Really secretive. They're called O.H.I.O."

"Like the state?" Darron asks, leaning into the coffee pot and taking a deep breath of the aroma that has just begun to percolate.

"That's the acronym. It stands for the Order of Human Improvement Options."

"That's ominous," Darron declares.

"I hadn't heard of them before last week, but they have pull. They set Jax up, killed Kit, and then got some poor sap to take the blame. Brent's not even in custody."

Darron nearly drops the cup he's holding in anticipation of his fresh coffee. "I saw Brent get arrested. That one cop, Detective Sloane, took him in."

"Detective McGinnis thinks that Sloane's being strong armed." McGinnis is one cop I trust; he's been nothing but straight with me. "Maybe his family is being threatened. I don't know. The point is Brent is free. He's not going to be punished for Kit's murder."

"Brent is free?" comes a tiny voice from behind me.

Shit. Shauna.

I turn slowly. "Shauna, I wanted to break it to you in a better way." Shauna is my sister-in-law. *Ex* sister in law. Jax's bio sister and part of the family into which Kit, as a fae changeling, was adopted.

I prepare for the worst. A tornado of righteous fae fury that can take down the house and us with it.

"My brother's killer is just walking around, being a total dick-wad, free and clear?" she asks, her small face scrunched in anger.

I nod hesitantly. "Brent's better connected than I imagined," I tell her.

She clenches and unclenches her fist. "I'm going to find him and kill him."

Finding him won't be a problem. He's running for the senate. He's very high profile. Killing him, though? Even after all the shit he put me through, I don't want him dead. I want him punished and to pay for his crimes.

"He's protected," I tell Shauna. "Going after him is a suicide mission."

"I've been on plenty of those," she says. I can see she's ready to flit off to exact murderous revenge.

Good thing Darron cuts in. "Maybe some coffee first?" he suggests, placing a steaming cup in front of me. "Shauna, I can blend yours with ice cream, just the way you like."

She sniffles. "Yeah, okay. Kit's not getting any deader."

I'm shocked at her nonchalance, but I know she's already cried and raged and drugged herself into oblivion. This is just the next item on her coping mechanism list.

She does put a hand on my bare arm as she walks by and for a moment I feel a tug of exhaustion. I slap her away.

"Don't you ever feed on me," I tell her, anger dripping from every word. Fae can feed on beauty. It gives them a nice high and their victim looks rundown and feels exhausted. Though there are no long-term effects for the fed-upon, I'm not going to fuel Shauna's appetites. Especially not if it means I have to feel like shit.

She pouts. "I need a little pick me up. I did just get some earth-shattering news. Besides, take it for the compliment it is."

"In case you forgot, I just had my world turned upside down, too," I tell her. "I took you in, gave you a place to stay. I am not enabling your addiction. And if you want to compliment me, feel free to do it with words. Like maybe a thank you?"

"Fine," she pouts. "There's a bridal fair at the convention center today. I'll stop by there and feed on all those bridezilla bitches."

Darron places her coffee milkshake in front of Shauna and sits. "Just make sure to step over the dead vamp on your way out."

"Another one?" Shauna looks at me, wide-eyed. "Paige, I never thought human lives were this interesting."

"Thanks," I say, settling in next to her as she shoves a powdered donut in her face.

"Want to come to the bridal con with me?" Shauna asks, spraying powder across the table.

"No, I really don't," I tell her. In another timeline, I would have accepted Brent's offer of marriage, and gone to that convention looking for dresses, floral arrangement ideas, and the perfect cake topper. But I'm living in this one, where my former fiancé is an underground criminal and my ex sister-in-law eats all my food.

My phone vibrates, and I sigh.

Also in this reality: a sexy, one-eyed werewolf detective waiting for me outside.

———

Continue reading **Grime & Punishment, Down & Dirty Book 2!**

SNEAK PEEK: FIRE & FLOOD (MYTHVERSE #1)

1

My parents and sister are at the airport, getting ready to board a plane headed toward Greece. Meanwhile, I'm waiting to be checked out of the hospital.

I'm supposed to be on that flight with them—a three-month work trip that my archeologist mom organized. But two weeks earlier I came down with a virus that turned into pneumonia. This, combined with my lifelong mortal enemy, asthma, made breathing suddenly a lot harder. And then nearly impossible.

That's where the hospital comes in.

The doctors saved my life. And then totally ruined it by telling my parents I should stay home tucked under a blanket on my grandmother's couch so I could be all rested up for my senior year of high school come fall.

I honestly didn't think they would really go without me. No offense to my grandma, but she's pretty old and kinda wobbly. No way would my parents leave their sickly daughter with her while they were on a totally different continent.

"Leave me behind? Screw that," I'd laughed right after the doctor who gave me the bad news left the room.

No one else laughed. Mom, Dad, and my older sister Mavis just stared back at me.

I swallowed, not liking those looks. "Right?"

"Well, sweetheart—" Mom paused as she took off her glasses and began to clean them on the hem of her shirt. It's one of her favorite avoidance tactics. When I was ten and asked her what sex was, she polished so long and hard that she snapped them in half.

Suddenly I was worried.

"Dad?" I turned to my no-bullshit go-to guy.

"Sweetheart, we rented out our house. Not to mention that for Mom, it's a work trip."

"And I'm getting college credits for an internship," Mavis added. That one really stung. Mavis and I have always been close. Sure there's the usual sisterly bickering, but beneath that we genuinely like each other. I was looking forward to spending the summer together exploring Greece with her and hearing about her first year of college out in California. All year she only came home for Christmas and I missed her like crazy. But now she's heading off again. Without me.

I argued—eloquently, I believe, or as eloquently as someone who has to suck on an inhaler when they get too worked up—for my right to go on this trip. Sure, it was about having fun, but it was also about education, and opportunity and... and the fact that I'd already rubbed it in all my ex-friends' faces that I was going.

In the end, we compromised. And by compromised I mean they just decided.

They would go to Greece as planned.

I would stay with Grandma and she would teach me

how to knit. Which was also, Mom pointed out, a learning opportunity. They presented me with a big cotton bag filled with a rainbow's worth of yarn and my very own pair of knitting needles.

It was one hell of a consolation prize. But I wasn't raised to be a sore loser, so I forced a smile and a thank you. Somehow I even managed to wish them well on their travels. Did an evil voice deep inside wish them months of chronic diarrhea? Maybe. But at least I didn't say it aloud.

Maybe I can knit them some diapers.

Now, I hold my bag of knitting supplies as a nurse wheels me out to the curb where my grandma waits behind the wheel of her '85 Lincoln. As I settle myself in the passenger seat my phone bings with a text.

MAVIS: We just boarded.

MAVIS: Didn't get seats together, but luckily I've already made friends.

A pic follows this second text. Mavis and some unbelievably good-looking guy grinning into the camera.

That is so typical Mavis. Even her bad luck turns out good. Stuck by herself and ends up next to one of the hottest guys in the universe.

The car jerks sideways and thumps up onto the curb and then down again. My phone flies out of my hand.

"Almost got that sonofabitch!" Grandma yells, giving her steering wheel a slap that I can't decide is meant to be congratulatory or an admonishment. I look back to see an alligator sunning himself beside the ditch at the side of the road. Gran hates them ever since they ate her Bichon Frise, Elsa, and attempts to mow them down with her car whenever possible. "Next time, next time," she mutters.

"Hey Grandma," I say, in my best poor pathetic left

behind tone of voice. "Maybe I can drive the rest of the way home? Get some practice in? It would really lift my spirits."

Grandma shoots me a look that is clearly meant to convey she may be seventy-three, but she ain't senile yet. "Sweetheart, you've failed that driving test what is it...eight times now? Didn't the last tester beg you to quit before you killed someone?"

"Grandma, I know how to drive," I protest. "I'm just a bad test taker."

I'm actually epically terrible. I tend to freeze up in high stress situations. And there is no situation more stressful than trying to go where you want without having to beg Mom or Dad for a lift.

"You're sick, Edie. What kind of grandma do you think I am? Why not rest a little bit on the way home? You look a little peaked." The light changes and Grandma floors it, slamming me back into my seat.

Another battle lost. It's true, though, I am tired. I close my eyes and try to pretend I'm on a plane. It's lifting up into the sky, to travel across an ocean, before finally settling down in the land where gods were born.

———

As we pull into the parking lot behind Grandma's condo the typical Florida afternoon downpour begins. Grandma slowly totters along while holding her little old lady umbrella that she always keeps in her handbag over my head so I don't get soaked and end up back in the hospital. It's nice and all, but I'm about three feet taller than Grandma so I end up just kind of walking hunched over to get under the umbrella, which doesn't make my chest feel too hot.

Finally we get into the creaky old elevator. It grumbles and lurches its way up to the sixth floor. By the time Grandma unlocks the door all I want to do is cry.

"What's that face for?" Dad asks.

I gasp. He's seated at Grandma's breakfast bar with a cup of coffee. Not on a plane to Greece—but here.

"You stayed!" I rush forward, throwing my arms around him. "I knew you wouldn't leave without me. Where are Mom and Mavis? Are they mad they missed their trip?"

The look on Dad's face as he peels away from me tells me everything I need to know. "Edie, it was Mom's grant. And her dream. You know that. Asking her to miss this chance..."

I swallow hard. Force a nod. "Right. I know."

And I do know. Mom met Dad when they were both studying abroad in Greece years ago. They fell in love, she got pregnant, and Mom decided to stay home with us kids and give up her career until we were older. I never really understood it. Why couldn't she do both?

When I ask Mom she'll only says she was overly worried about our safety just like any young mom. Really, though, Dad's always been the more overprotective one, while Mom is constantly pushing me to let go and embrace my wild side. I've tried to tell her I don't have a wild side, that I'm pretty sure I was born without one. That's when she gets this glint in her eye and insists that someday I'm going to surprise myself. If Mavis is around she always like to add, "In bed." Ha ha ha, Mavis.

Anyway, once I started high school, Mom decided it was time to pick up where she left off. She finished her degree and then this opportunity to work in Greece came up. Dad didn't like it. They tried to hide the fact they were arguing, but even though neither of them are screamers, there's always a certain tone to their voices when they're upset. Eventually Mom won and well, it was immediately obvious how excited she was. Suddenly Greece this and Greece that was all Mom could talk about.

So yeah, unless I was on my deathbed, there's no way Mom wasn't getting on that airplane. And Mavis, well, she was always Mom's favorite, while I've always been Dad's.

I hug Dad again. "Thank you for coming back for me."

He ruffles my hair. Or tries. It's wet, so he just sort of rubs my head instead. "Well, I had to decide who needed more help staying out of trouble—you or your mom. You won, but only just barely."

"Hey, Dad," I smile up at him. "Speaking of trouble... since we're here all summer with nothing to do, maybe you can help me get more driving practice in."

"Aw, baby girl." Dad smiles fondly. "I would rather spend an afternoon wrestling alligators than be inside a vehicle you're driving."

"Dad!"

"But I did have an idea." He rummages in his pocket and then holds up two laminated cards with a ta-da expression.

"Those are bus passes."

"Yup. Good all summer. I figured, well, maybe we could explore the public transportation system in our fair city. It's eco-friendly and it'll be an adventure!"

I stare at Dad. He is working so hard to sell this. Only the vice principal of a junior high school would be this excited about bus passes, and only a monster would burst his bubble.

"Wow. Bus passes and knitting. Best summer ever." Somehow I manage to keep most of the sarcasm out of my voice.

Dad grins back at me. "Best summer ever," he echoes.

Thing is, I think he means it.

———

Keep reading for FREE! Download Fire & Flood Now!

SNEAK PEEK: THE MIDLIFE LADY'S GUIDE TO A BAD HOROSCOPE (POWERS OF THE ZODIAC PREQUEL)

1

I know that I'm not the first bride to be left standing at the altar with no groom in sight. It's almost a cliché — one that's always played for laughs—and usually gets them.

I'm not laughing.

But I am *smiling*, because I am Madison Thorne and Madison Thorne is always smiling. You can see it in my Facebook posts with my beautiful family, my Instagram pics with my latest to-die-for crafting idea, and in the Pinterest board of ideas I made for this special day.

Except I had always imagined that my husband would be next to me.

Okay, maybe I *am* laughing. It's a slightly hysterical giggle—there's a limit to grace under pressure. Because here's the thing: while a bride can get stood up on her wedding day by a groom with cold feet...how many women deal with a no-show husband for a vow *renewal* ceremony?

I give the minister a piece of my strained smile. We're not regular churchgoers, really, just Christmas and Easter with the family. But this minister married us twenty-five years ago and I thought it would be nice to have him perform our vow renewal, even though there's nothing religious about it. We're not even having our ceremony in a church. We're in a beautiful forest—my idea—and the spring breeze rushing past me is comforting.

Well, kind of.

About twelve years ago a cataclysmic event sent shock waves through the entire world. Natural disasters erupted everywhere, food chain supplies were broken, and it kind of felt like the apocalypse for a little bit. But the biggest shock by far was that it turned out all of the paranormal creatures we'd thought were myths were actually quite real. Vampires, werewolves, pixies, and all kinds of bizarre creatures came out of the woodwork, and it took some time for humans to adapt to the new normal.

Things were a bit hairy for a while. Some of the supes made gangs, claimed territory, and then moved on to terrorizing everyone in the vicinity. We were lucky to live in a neighborhood that was spared from the worst of it. But the church we were married in was not so fortunate. Apparently some fae fire balls went astray when they were fighting a gang of vampires. The interior of the church went up in flames, leaving only the brick shell standing. Last I heard a pack of harpy meth-heads are squatting there.

Honestly, I'm not too broken up about not being able to recreate the "I dos" we exchanged inside that dark old building. In my memories of that day, I recall feeling trapped and boxed in. I was young and powerless. It never occurred to me that I could have a say in my own destiny. Of course, it all worked out. But still, it feels good to be the one steering the ship this time.

If only I could've steered Bert's ship too, maybe he would be here right now.

With that thought, I glance over my shoulder.

Everyone I know is here...minus my husband. My parents, my kids, friends, family. And they're all looking at me with various levels of pity in their eyes. Well, no, actually, my youngest boy, Oliver, hasn't looked up from his phone. The signal out here isn't great, but I guess he doesn't need it for that shooting game he loves.

Love. Yeah. My monosyllabic son definitely loves his computer games. It's the only topic where I can get more than one-word answers from him. Once Ollie was so excited about a new skin he bought, he waxed poetic about it for a full ten minutes. I had no idea what he was talking about, but I feigned enthusiasm for his sake—after first Googling to figure out what a skin was, and hoping that my youngest wasn't wandering into some weird internet sex thing.

'Cause that's love too. Isn't it?

You take an interest in the things your loved one cares about. It's a form of showing up, even if in this instance it was only me murmuring, "Oooh," "Wow," and "Yeah, of course you should get the beheading emote."

My husband Bert is terrible at showing up in these small ways. Instead, he's the master of the grand gesture. Like a wedding renewal ceremony in front of all our friends and family.

That's how I know this is not a case of cold feet. Bert and I have been married for twenty-five years. And this whole renewal thing was his idea. He'd wanted to give me the ceremony in the woods that I'd always dreamed about—instead of the stuffy church wedding that my parents provided when I was eighteen and had a bun in the oven.

The thought of the reception dinner at the ancient firemen's hall with three hundred of our not-so-closest friends and relatives still makes me cringe. It had sticky floors and reeked of old booze and stale beer. It didn't help that I was nauseous the whole time and trying desperately to suck in my baby bump. I'd smiled through it all, though.

So here we are, in a clearing that the park service rents out for events. I had to work hard to not make it look like a summer camp pow-wow. I cleaned out the fire pit, raked all of the leaves and sticks for at least half an acre, and set up soft lighting. White Christmas lights were in the discount bin and they look lovely wound around the trees, and if a few pixies are hovering around them it just adds to the ambience. I know that particular types of supe—what people call the supernaturals—are attracted to lights, so the Christmas bulbs are doing double duty.

I even put mosquito lures in the forest in a one-mile radius so all annoying bugs would be drawn to them and leave our guests alone. As usual, I've thought of everything.

There was no sound system so I rented a generator and got the DJ set up ahead of time, all the while praying that it wouldn't rain. I got a great deal on renting a few hundred white chairs from the church, but they were a bit dingy so I got them to knock off the price if I painted them all. I even hand-stenciled a small lily onto the backrest of each one, adding a nice floral touch that can also be religious for when the chairs go back to their rightful owners.

I didn't want to spend the money on catering so I cooked everything myself, including three hundred mini cakes. Each one was hand frosted by yours truly with a heart and *Maddie & Bert* lovingly written in pink buttercream. I think I gave myself carpal tunnel—either that or I am clutching this bouquet way too hard. I force myself to relax and hope that the tension from my hands didn't go up into my smile. It needs to look natural, just like everything else out here. Everything for my perfect day.

It was worth all the work. I came in way under budget. Not that Bert gave me one. He actually specifically told me not to pinch pennies. But Bert doesn't balance the checkbook. I do. And right now...things are tight. I know it'll all turn out okay, somehow it always does. Just when it seems like we won't be able to pay the mortgage, Bert returns from Southern France—or some other equally exotic destination—with a new antique that he sells for an amount big enough to make all our dreams come true...for a while at least.

I could make one of those checks last a lifetime. But Bert's dreams are too big. And expensive. He says that's why we make a perfect team. His head is in the clouds while my feet are on the ground. And he's right; we've gone through twenty-five years this way. It's just that sometimes...

With a sigh, I lift my head to the sky, it's clear and the full moon hangs low, visible even though night is hours away. Someone was telling me something about this moon...it was a blood moon or something. I can't remember. Maybe tonight after the guests leave and it's just me and Bert we can turn off all the lights and lay under the night sky to stargaze...and then maybe direct our attention elsewhere.

Beside me, the minister clears his throat. The last twenty-five years haven't been kind to him; he needs a cane to stay upright and is looking deeply uncomfortable. "It's been thirty-five minutes..." he tells me. His tone is apologetic, but there's an edge that wasn't in his voice when we first realized that Bert was missing. Then he said, "Renewal ceremonies are such joyous occasions. Like so many of the best things in life, they're worth waiting for." I guess, like everyone, the minister has limits.

"Just five more minutes," I say. The same as I've said six

times now. I hope my smile still looks genuine, and I'm not showing too many teeth. Even if I did have them whitened just for the occasion.

His lips compress, but then he nods. I know that I won't get another five minutes after this. If Bert doesn't show soon this minister will be walking—or, em, shuffling—away.

Darn it, Bert!

I smooth down my dress—a beautiful retro piece from the seventies that I found at a garage sale while looking for the vintage clothing shop—and sigh once more.

My Bert. I've told him so many times that he packs his days too full. He's a man who is hungry for life. He wants to experience everything. It's what I love about him. But also, after twenty plus years, it's what leads to most of my frustrations with him. He's never on time, dashing in at the last possible minute for parent-teacher conferences. Or showing up fashionably late to parties being thrown in our own backyard. Once he was in charge of bringing the welcome bags, and showed up just in time to give them to guests as they were leaving.

And it's not that he forgets. It's always, "I'm sorry baby, I got hung up..."

He's a businessman. Always making deals, meeting new people, cementing old friendships, and then selling something to them. And he financially supports our family—as he reminds me more often than is altogether necessary. There's a little flare of anger in my stomach at the thought, and I have to work hard to keep my smile in place. The minister clears his throat and I know it's time to get this party started—without the groom.

Unlike the first time around, this is *my day*. And nothing —not even my husband—is going to ruin it for me.

I turn to face my family and friends. "We all know Bert;

he probably spotted a piece of artwork in the airport that is worth more than anyone ever thought, and is currently haggling with the art director—who will be his new best friend after some drinks. So let's go ahead and celebrate, and we can do the ceremony later!" I say, with a huge smile.

There is a collective sigh of relief. I make sure the minister gets a chair so he can rest, give a wave to the DJ to let him know to start spinning, and put the fairy lights on twinkle mode, which brings in a few more pixies and makes for a festive atmosphere. I assure everyone that I'm fine; it's just an unexpected delay. I move from group to group, smiling like my life depends on it.

I read once that a scientific study showed that the physical act of smiling can actually help lift a person's mood. Now, though, I have to wonder exactly how they knew this. I'd lie through my upturned lips that this is a perfect day and that my every smile only increases my joy. And if they called me on it, I'd only smile harder.

"Mom, are you okay?" my oldest, Nathan, asks. How am I old enough to have a twenty-four-year old child?! He's already in grad school. An actual adult. I am old enough to have three adult children. Even number four, the baby, is now in high school! Nathan sees the stricken look on my face and misunderstands—he thinks I'm upset with his father. And of course I'm not. Of course I'm not mad at Bert. Of course not.

"Yes, you know your father," I say with a wave of my hand.

"He doesn't deserve you," he mumbles. "He takes you for granted." My heart twists for my little boy, even if he is all grown up now. Once he worshipped the ground Bert walked on. But too many years of missed baseball games, debate finals, and even his college graduation has put a strain on their relationship. I make a note to have Bert invite him for a guy's night out. They'll have some drinks together and Bert will smooth things over until Nathan forgets all about those old hurts. Well...mostly.

"Marriage is work," I tell him, giving his arm a little squeeze. "You'll understand one day."

"Sure. Mom, get some food," he says. But I probably won't. There's a feeling in my stomach that doesn't mix well with food. Disappointment. My face still apparently isn't doing a great job of conveying absolute joy, because Nathan's glower deepens.

I decide it's time to change the subject. "Do you know who that man is over there?" I point to a tall dark-haired man who slipped into the party late. Irrationally, I'm a bit annoyed at this stranger—not for crashing my party, but for giving me a moment's hope that Bert had finally arrived.

Nathan frowns. "I saw Aunt Stephy hanging on him earlier..." he says.

"Oh, okay," I say, since that pretty much answers it all.

My younger sister Stephanie is a triple divorcée on the hunt for number four. Which is fine. To each their own. I'm not here to judge her choices. But it's a bit annoying that she refuses to extend the same courtesy to me. She's made it very clear that she thinks this whole vow renewal ceremony is lame and cheesy and—worst of all—smug.

Well, I bet she's loving how things turned out. There's nothing to be smug about now.

Again, Nathan must see something of what I'm thinking, because he curls his hands into fists. "When Dad shows up I'm going to..."

"You won't do anything," I cut him off. "You won't ruin the party."

"Dad already did that," he shoots back, but he won't

cause a fuss. He knows I would hate that. Any type of confrontation is absolutely not my thing. Bert likes to talk about how we never fight. Ever. He does a whole little bit about it when we meet new people.

"This is my wife, Maddie," he says, a twinkle in his eyes. "I know the name paired with that wild curly hair of hers makes her look like a lady with a temper. But believe it or not, we've never had a single fight. And it's not because I'm a perfect saint either. Or no, I could *tempt* a saint." He pauses here for knowing laughter from those familiar with him— and almost everyone is. Then he continues, "But my Maddie here, she never gets mad."

Then it's my turn to give the punchline, "I never get mad, but someday I might get even."

Every single time Bert reacts like it's his first time hearing it. His eyes pop wide and he startles back, a hand to his heart. "Uh-oh," he cries as the laughter around us grows louder. "I better watch myself then!'

I always laugh along. But I have to say, I've noticed that he never joins in. Instead, he smiles and takes a drink, always surveying those around us to make sure he's doing his job of making everyone like him. Sometimes when I see him reading the room like that it sends a chill up my spine...and not always a good one. He always knows how to get exactly the right reaction out of people, and how to get what he wants from them. Lord knows he's got me. Smiling, Maddie "Never Mad" Thorne.

But really this might be the last straw. Maybe this time I won't shove my feelings down. Maybe this time I'll curse him out and threaten to...

I don't know what I'd do. I've put so much work into being perfectly nice that I don't even know how to get angry. And it's not like I could ever throw something at Bert, stamp my foot and demand an apology—I've never had to. He always walks in the door with the right words, and I can't resist a man who isn't afraid to say he's sorry.

I've loved Robert Thorne for as long as I can remember.

"Mom!" the twins call to me. "Come dance!"

I plaster on a smile and go to them. They are a perfectly adorable pair, with matching faces that somehow look great on both a boy and a girl. In family pictures we always look fantastic, even if Bert is sometimes a little flushed from running into the studio fifteen minutes behind schedule.

The music is lovely as it bounces off the trees and flows through the evening air, the pixies bobbing up and down along with it. It's getting darker, and we'll have to pay some attention to make sure there aren't any harpies or vampires lurking in the higher branches of the trees, but the park service does a pretty good job of keeping public areas free of some of the more violent supes. In fact, I had raided the cash register at my vintage clothing store to slip the rangers a few extra twenties to keep them on the party perimeter after sunset, just in case.

I had a plan, and I wasn't going to let anything ruin my perfect night.

But I didn't plan on my husband being a no-show.

Continue reading **The Midlife Lady's Guide to a Bad Horoscope!**

him even though interspecies dating is taboo. I think he might like me too...even though I did accidentally set him on fire the first time we met. Awkward!

It's not all fun and games, though. MOA has a darker side and the more time I spend here, the more secrets I uncover. And the worst secret of all just might be about me.

Fire & Flood is a young adult magic academy fantasy novel with non-stop action. It contains a spunky heroine, one best friend with the gift of sight...to see tomorrow's lunch menu, a mean-girl vampire roommate with a carnivorous plant, and a meet-cute with her roommate's hot twin brother that almost kills them both.

Read the first book for FREE!

————

Three women experience their midlife crisis in the worst way - by finding out they are all married to the same man.

Their shared husband deals with magical artifacts, and has hidden three pieces of a *talentum dei* - a magical object that can deliver the powers of a god to its handler - with each of his wives. When the three women accidentally meet and the *talentum* assembles, they are each given a power that matches their star sign, and their husband - intent on having power for himself - makes a grab for the *talentum*, only to have it kill him. The three - very different - women find themselves imbued with powers, suddenly single, and on the run from powerful people who are after the *talentum*... with the ghost of their shared dead husband along for the ride.

The Midlife Lady's Guide to a Bad Horoscope is available now!

ABOUT THE AUTHORS

DEMITRIA LUNETTA is the author of the YA books THE FADE, BAD BLOOD, and the sci-fi duology, IN THE AFTER and IN THE END. She is also an editor and contributing author for the YA anthology, AMONG THE SHADOWS: 13 STORIES OF DARKNESS & LIGHT. Find her at www.demitrialunetta.com for news on upcoming projects and releases.

KATE KARYUS QUINN is an avid reader and menthol chapstick addict with a BFA in theater and an MFA in film and television production. She lives in Buffalo, New York with her husband, three children, and one enormous dog. She has three young adult novels published with HarperTeen: ANOTHER LITTLE PIECE, (DON'T YOU) FORGET ABOUT ME, AND DOWN WITH THE SHINE. She also recently released her first adult novel, THE SHOW MUST GO ON, a romantic comedy. Find out more at www.katekaryusquinn.com

MARLEY LYNN is a lost child of the gods, who waits on the shores of Lake Erie for her parents to bring her home. In the meantime, she contents herself with reading, writing, and gardening. Find out more at www.MarleyLynn.com

ACKNOWLEDGMENTS

Thank you to Marin McGinnis for taking care of our copy edits!

And, of course, a big thank you to our families for putting up with us crazy writers.